WHEN A DOOR CLOSES

J L Coates

Library and Archives Canada in Publication

J L Coates

ISBN: 978-1-7751668-4-9

Printed in USA by KDP

Cover photo by Google Stock

BOOKS BY THE AUTHOR

Judith Coates – Be Who You Be

Let Your Light Shine

my life, my story with Beyond the

Heart Clubhouse

Extraordinary Time of Good vs Evil

J L Coates – Second Chances

Awakening

Two Women, Two Stories

Shattered

The Seeker, the Sentinel and the Orb

Total Equals the Sum of the Parts

A Change of Heart

Journeys

DEDICATION

For David

ACKNOWLEDGEMENTS

Thank you once again to my amazing team, Editor Dianne Tchir and Beta reader Clarice Nelson.

Together you are somehow able to take my words and mold them into what I am trying to say.

Thank you to my many readers for showing their appreciation for my writing in so many ways.

This is a work of fiction. No person, place or event is anything other than a product of my overactive imagination.

Loss in any form is a deep, personal and often an overwhelming experience. If you are having trouble I encourage you to seek out any resources in your area, - Mental health, family physician, Church leader, local support groups or a trusted friend. "Talking helps, but sharing does too."

I do not define myself by how many roadblocks have
appeared in my path

I define myself by the courage I've found to forge new
roads.

I do not define myself by how many disappointments I've
faced

I define myself by the forgiveness and the faith I found to
begin again.

I do not define myself by how long a relationship lasted.

I define myself by how much I have loved, and been willing
to love again.

I do not define myself by how many times I have been
knocked down.

I define myself by how many times I have struggled to my
feet

I am not my pain.

I am not my past.

I am that which emerged from the fire.

Author unknown

From the internet

PROLOGUE

My name is Lucille Ellen Barnes. My friends call me Lucy and I was named after both of my grandmothers. This is my story. I have heard people say if your life is filled with lemons, make lemonade, but sometimes that's not always possible. Strangely enough what we think might happen, and what actually does, are totally different. Just when I thought I had life figured out, it threw me a curve.

First of all, I just turned forty two years old and was married to my husband, Jim, for twenty five years. All that time I was a stay at home mom, my family was my life.

I am short, just a little over five feet, slightly overweight, have mousey brown hair with some gray intermixed which I usually wear in a ponytail and wear heavy black rimmed glasses to make my face look less round.

Jim and I had three children – twin girls Amy and Angie, born six months after we were married and a son Donnie, who is two years younger than the girls. I know what you are thinking and you are right, but that's a small part of my story.

Jim didn't make an excessive amount of money, but we always seemed to manage. To be honest, I have no idea how much he actually made, because every month he gave me a generous allowance for groceries and whatever extra I needed for the kids.

Then one day everything changed. The happy contented life I was living turned out to be a lie. I ended up widowed, alone, disillusioned, broke, and my children hated me. I worked for minimum wage to pay for my apartment and fell in love with a man three years younger than me

.   Today I easily tell my story about how, from the ashes of bitterness and despair, a new life can be experienced but, at one time, my life was a living hell, I learned that all one has to do is take a chance on herself. Love is about taking a risk and letting go of the fear and self-recriminations. I believe if I can overcome these odds, you can handle anything life throws at you. I know because I did it.

CHAPTER ONE

The day my life changed started the same as every other. I liked to get up early, have my morning coffee and write in my journal. My husband Jim is a foreman for Atlas Road Maintenance. He started at the bottom and worked his way up until now he had twenty mechanics working under him. As usual he worked late the night before and I was half asleep when he crawled into bed.

"You still awake Lucy?" He asked.

"Sort of," I mumbled.

"I'm not feeling very well. I've never had a headache like this before. I feel like my head is going to explode. I'm off tomorrow so I'm going to sleep in. Maybe I will feel better in the morning."

"Can I get you something for the pain?"

"No, I had a stressful day. I'm tired that's all this is."

"Whatever" I mumbled and rolled over. I never gave his complaint a second thought. If I had it might have changed the outcome, but I will never know.

This wasn't like Jim, but I put his headache down to the fact he was working a lot of overtime shifts because the company was short staffed.

I was on my second cup of coffee when I heard him call out. "Lucy, help me." followed by a loud thump on the floor. I raced down the hallway and up the stairs. When I got to our bedroom Jim was lying on the floor, gasping for breath, and clutching his head with both hands.

I froze and stared at him. "What are you doing down there?" I asked.

"Don't just stand there, call an ambulance," he gasped, and then his eyes rolled back into his head.

I felt strangely calm as I dialed 9 -1-1 and gave them the details and our address. Then I sat on the floor beside Jim and cradled his head in my lap. I was numb. I couldn't understand what was happening to him.

The ambulance arrived and when he was stable, the attendants loaded him into the back. I rode in the front with the driver, and the other attendant stayed with Jim. As soon as we arrived at the emergency department doors he was whisked away, and I was left to deal with the paper work. Then, not knowing what else to do, I sat in the waiting room and waited for somebody to come and tell me what was happening with my husband. I don't remember grabbing my purse on the way out the door, but I had it with me.

I sat there for what seemed like hours. After a while, one of the nurses took pity on me and led me to a consultation room.

"Can I get you anything Mrs. Barnes? Maybe a cup of coffee?"

"No thank you. Can you tell me what is wrong with my husband? What are they doing for his headache?" I couldn't have swallowed it anyway. The mere thought made me feel sick to my stomach.

"I don't exactly know but I am sure the doctor will come to update you any minute."

Anxiously I stood at the door of the room watching the hallway until I saw our family doctor, Kyle Richards walking toward me. The look on his face scared me.

"How are you holding up Lucy?" he asked."

"Never mind me, how is Jim? What happened?"

"He has a leaking aneurysm in his brain. I have called for the Life Support helicopter to take him to the city. We need to get him there as quickly as possible."

"Can't you help him here?" I asked. Now, when I think back, I realize that was a stupid question. If they could have helped him here they would be doing so.

"We are doing all we can, but we aren't equipped for that specialized kind of surgery. The helicopter should be here in about thirty minutes and I am going to with him. How about I take you to his room and you can sit with him until we are ready to go?"

"I would like that." I replied.

As we walked down the hall he explained what was happening in Jim's head by comparing a blood vessel to a tire. "Sometimes the air leaks out slowly and the tire can be fixed, other times it blows out while a person is driving. In Jim's case I am hoping the blood is leaking slowly, and we will be in time to fix it. There is no way to be sure until he is on the operating room table. A neuro surgeon is on standby and will take Jim to the O R the minute the helicopter lands."

I went into Jim's room. He was hooked up to an I. V., a heart monitor and there was an oxygen cannula in his nose. His eyes were closed, but his hands were in constant motion, clutching and unclutching the sheet.

I took one of his hands in mine. "I am here Jim. Hang on. We are waiting for a helicopter to take you to Central City University Hospital for surgery. Kyle Richardson is going with you in the plane, and I will get Donnie to drive me. I will get there as soon as I can."

Jim opened his eyes. Grimacing with pain he whispered, "My head hurts Lucy. Stay with me."

"Please Jim, don't talk. I'm not going any place, I will be right here until it is time for you to go, then be at your bedside when you open your eyes."

"The kids...."

"I haven't had a chance to tell them yet. The next time a nurse comes in I'll ask her to call Donnie, and then he can call the girls. I doubt if they will have time to get here before you leave."

I sat beside him praying. Then his eyes opened again. "I'm sorry Lucy. I love you more than you know. I really made a mess of things. Please forgive me, I didn't mean to hurt you. I thought I would have time to fix my mistakes."

I had no idea what he was talking about. "You have nothing to be sorry for Jim Barnes. I love you too and have for a very long time. In a few days we will look back on this and put it into the past where it belongs." Tears rolled down my face and I didn't try to wipe them away.

"Please don't cry," he said, and then his eyes closed again.

I squeezed his hand. "Rest now, the helicopter should be here any minute."

In the next few minutes his breathing slowed and then stopped. "Open your eyes Jim." I pleaded. "Look at me. Please Jim, don't leave me," I begged, but I knew he was gone forever.

At the same time I heard excited voices in the hallway. Dr. Richards came into the room followed by two paramedics pushing a stretcher.

"We are ready to go now," he said, and the paramedics pushed the stretcher to the side of the bed.

"It's too late." I said, "He is gone."

Dr. Richards pulled the stethoscope from around his neck and put it on Jim's chest "Call a code blue."

He pushed me out of the way, jumped up on the side of

the bed and began to do heart compressions. The resuscitation team ran into the room and they worked frantically for another ten minutes to get Jim's heart beating again.

"Stop Dr. Richards," I said "It's too late."

He stopped and then listened to Jim's heart again. "Yes it is Lucy. I don't know for sure if we would have made it in time or not. I am so sorry. Would you like to stay with him for a few minutes?"

"Yes," I answered. I was still trying to wrap my head around how Jim could be talking to me one minute and be dead the next. Nothing was making any sense.

The paramedics pushed the stretcher out of the room and they all left. I sat down again beside the bed and picked up Jim's hand again. "Please come back to me. I don't know how to live without you. The kids and I need you." I begged, but knew my pleas were useless.

A few minutes later a nurse came in, removed Jim's I. V. and the oxygen tube from his nose, and turned off the heart monitor. Silence filled the room.

"You can stay with him as long as you want," She said.

I sat beside the bed holding Jim's hand in both of mine. I put his hand to my lips, kissed it one more time, then tucked it under the covers and pulled the blankets up under his chin. That's how he liked to sleep. I was alone; too stunned to comprehend that my husband was dead.

After a while the nurse came back on into the room and put her hand on my shoulder. "Mrs. Barnes, can I call someone for you?"

"Yes please. Call my son Donnie and ask him to come get me."

"Come Mrs. Barnes, there is nothing more you can do here."

I knew she was right. I kissed Jim's lips one last time. "Good bye my darling," I whispered into his ear, "I will love you forever."

I turned to the nurse and asked her, "What do I do from here?"

She led me to a small lounge located by the nurse's station, left and then returned with a cup of tea. "I called your son, he is on his way. I told him his father had unexpectedly passed away and that you were here."

"Thank you," I replied. "That must have been a difficult call for you to make I appreciate your kindness." She patted my arm and left the room. I remember that I kept staring at a picture on the wall of three horses frolicking in the ocean. I was numb. I couldn't think.

Soon I heard Donnie's voice in the room with me. He was pale, his face contorted in pain. He wrapped his arms around me and said, "Come on mom, let's go home. Angie and Amy will be at the house waiting for us."

"Do you want to see your dad before we leave?"

"I already did," he replied, his voice cracking with emotion. "He looks peaceful; as though he is sleeping."

I didn't say anything. Donnie put his arm around my shoulders, and we began to walk down the hall. I stopped. I turned to go back to Jim's room, but he pulled me back.

"I can't leave him here all alone," I said. "I have to stay with him. What will he think if I just walk away and leave him here?"

"Its okay mom, the nurses will take good care of him."

I remember how confidently and gently he spoke to me. I looked at him, "What do we do now?"

"I don't know mom, but I am sure we will figure it out," he replied. "

I don't remember the drive home but when we got to the house the girls came rushing toward us. They were distraught. Both threw their arms around me. I remember I was shaking. I held them in my arms as any mother would, but I didn't feel anything. I remember telling them we would be alright.

"I need to sit down." I told them

Donnie took my arm, walked with me into the house, and led me to my favorite chair in the living room. After I sat down, he tucked a blanket around my legs.

"Can I get you something mom?

"No, I'm good," I replied.

I heard Amy tell Donnie, "Dr. Richard's phoned and wants you to call him back. He said dad died from a brain aneurysm and there was nothing they could do here. He also wants to know if we want an autopsy. Unless the doctor is sure of the cause of death, the law requires that it needs to be done but dad could be considered an exception to that rule."

I interrupted her. "No. I am sure he knew what he was doing. I trust he is telling the truth, besides it's not going to change anything."

How can this be? He never complained, and I would have known if he was sick. Did he know something was wrong and didn't tell me, or was he as surprised as I was? What was he talking about? What kind of mess has he left behind, and why was he saying he was sorry?

CHAPTER TWO

One of the girls must have called my best friend Cee Cee because she was the first person to arrive at the house. We became best friends in grade three and have remained that way ever since.

She was a year younger than me, a career woman, never married and never had any children. She owned her own company, travelled the world and, through the years, had a variety of lovers. Cee Cee never saw any sense in being tied down to one man. Sometimes I think I lived vicariously through her. Although in many ways we were total opposites, she was the one person I could count on to be there for me if I needed her.

"Aww honey," she said as she walked into the living room. She knelt down beside my chair wrapped her arms around me. "Angie phoned to tell me the news. I'm so sorry."

I buried my head in her hair. "Help me Cee Cee. I don't know if I can handle this."

"We will figure things out as we go along. Do you have any idea what happened?"

"Dr. Richards said he had a brain aneurysm. He was going to move him to the city for an operation, but it was too late."

"Has he been sick Lucy? Was he complaining of any pain?"

"When he got home from work last night, he said he wasn't feeling well and had a headache. He planned on sleeping in this morning because it was his day off. He was putting in a lot of long hours, and sometimes we didn't see each other for days. I would be asleep when he got home, and he was usually gone by the time I got up."

"Look honey. You've had a long hard day. Put your head back and try to relax. I am here and will help you as much as I can. Do you have any idea what kind of a service he wanted?"

"He didn't want a church service, just something small at the funeral home. He wanted to be cremated and buried beside his mom and dad. Strangely we talked about that not so long ago. Do you think he had a premonition?"

"No honey, I think it was simply talk between a husband and his wife, a passing conversation. Last question Lucy. We have to phone a funeral home do you have any one particular in mind?"

"Not really. Williams and Sons did his mother's funeral and it was quite nice."

"I'll ask Donnie to call them and start making the arrangements."

Cee Cee called Donnie to come into the room. "Donnie, I want you to look after the funeral arrangements. Cee Cee will be here to help you. Call Williams and Sons and ask if they are willing to look after the service for us. If they are, we have to let the hospital know."

"Do you have a day in mind mom? They will probably want to know."

"Saturday will be good. That gives us three days to do whatever we need to."

My head was pounding furiously. I leaned back against the chair and closed my eyes.

As word of Jim's passing got out, the house began to fill with people – our friends, Jim's boss and co-workers, neighbors, and I don't know who else. People came over, hugged me and offered their condolences. I felt as though I was in a fog – their voices were muffled and I couldn't see them clearly.

I heard the kids answering their questions. "No he wasn't sick. We are as shocked as you are. Yes, I will let you know when the funeral is." It was like a wave of words that didn't make any sense washing over me.

I remember thinking *I can't allow myself to cry because if I start, I don't know if I will be able to stop. I have to be strong for my children and grandchildren.*

Now, I know that was a mistake. My reaction left some people wondering if I had any feelings for Jim. They simply didn't understand.

Hours later Cee Cee came to me. "I sent the kids home and everyone else is gone. There is just the two of us. Now let's go upstairs and put you into bed. You are exhausted."

"No, I want to sleep down here tonight."

"You will rest better in your bed Lucy."

"I can't go up there. I can still see him lying on the floor, his eyes pleading for help."

Instead of arguing, Cee Cee went upstairs and got a pair of pajamas from my drawer. After I changed, she put a pillow on the couch and covered me with another blanket.

"I'll be right here if you need me."

I couldn't sleep, but I did lay there with my eyes closed. Once I opened them and looked at her. "I don't think I can do this."

"Do what honey?"

"Bury Jim and spend the rest of my life without him."

"The way I see it, you don't have any choice."

I hated that fact that she was always practical "I guess not, but I would give anything to have awakened this morning to another normal day."

She didn't answer me. I mean what could she say? We both knew I would never have that kind of normal again.

CHAPTER THREE

When I think back, I have a hard time remembering the events of the next few days. I know I kept waiting for Jim to walk through the door and then I would know this was a bad dream. I know my kids were worried about me. I heard Amy ask Cee Cee, "When is she going to cry? This isn't good for her."

"She will when she is ready," Cee Cee answered. "I think she is trying to be strong for the three of you."

They didn't understand. I felt that if I started crying for Jim he would be dead. I don't know how to explain my thinking at the time. Later, when I attended Grief Counselling sessions, I learned this was the first stage of the Grief process known as denial.

One time I took Donnie aside. "Please don't get carried away with your dad's funeral arrangements. Keep the cost down as much as possible."

"What do you mean mom?"

"Your dad would want things as simple as possible, besides I don't know if he had money set aside to pay for something like this. He never mentioned anything to me."

He looked at me strangely, "I didn't think about that."

We had Jim cremated like he wanted and a simple service at the funeral home. Donnie asked the United Church minister to do the service and Jim's boss, Ken Smith, to do the eulogy.

He spoke about Jim's sense of humor, his willingness to teach and help his employees, and the fact that he never appeared flustered, and always came across as calm, cool and collected.

Others spoke about Jim, and I was surprised to learn things about him I didn't know even after twenty-five years of marriage. What was clear was the love and respect they had for him.

The small chapel was packed and some had to stand at the back. I knew almost everybody that attended except for a small group of men. .I shouldn't have been surprised because Jim made friends easily. No matter where we went, he always stopped to talk to somebody.

We buried his ashes in the same grave as his mother. Afterwards the girls made arrangements for one of the local service groups to provide lunch at the community hall.

. Once the crowd of well-wishers began to thin out I insisted the girl's go home to be with their families and sent Donnie off to be with his friends. Naturally they argued with me.

"Mom, are you sure? We don't think it is good for you to be alone." Amy protested.

"I won't be alone. Cee Cee will be with me. Your husband and children are hurting too and you need to be with them."

After everybody left Cee Cee drove me back to the house. While she tidied up the kitchen and put the dirty dishes in the dishwasher. I lay down on the couch "Go home Cee Cee you have gone above the call of duty, but you need to get some rest too."

"Are you sure you want to be alone tonight?"

"I will be fine. There have been so many people around all the time, and so much confusion that I need some peace and quiet. I need time to think about what to do from here."

"Not tonight you don't. That can wait, what you need is some sleep. Promise me you will call if you need me."

"I have you on speed dial," I replied, holding my cell phone up to show her.

"Trust you to always have a smart answer."

"Go home, I'll be fine."

After she left, I changed out of my good clothes into one of Jim's t-shirts and an old pair of black yoga pants. I made myself a cup of tea and went back to the living room and plopped down on the couch. I was exhausted, and my head ached. I drank my tea and listened to the silence.

At some point I must have fallen asleep because I woke up feeling overwhelmed and filled with feelings of dread. My headache was worse. I was shaking. I felt as though there was a tight band around my chest and I couldn't catch my breath. I wondered if I was having a heart attack.

I reached for the phone and hit Cee Cee's number. "Hurry," I gasped, "I think I am having a heart attack."

"I am on my way," she replied, and her phone went dead. Every time I sat down and tried to relax I had the urge to get up and move.

When Cee Cee arrived she took one look at me. "I'm going to phone for an ambulance."

"No, we will go in your car. It will be faster."

By the time we arrived at the hospital, the tight band around my chest had loosened some and I felt a little calmer.

The Emergency room nurse was very efficient. She took me into a cubicle, handed me a gown and asked me to change. Then she hooked me up to an ECG machine for a heart tracing and put an oxygen mask on my face. "Big deep breaths" she told me, "breathe in slowly to the count of five and exhale slowly." A lab technician came in and took several vials of blood.

It took everything I had to lay in that room. It was the same one they had taken Jim into.

"Please Mrs. Barnes you must try to relax," the nurse kept insisting." Your blood pressure is very high and we don't want you to have a stroke." I tried, but it was difficult. I felt like I was going to jump out of my skin.

After Cee Cee gave them my information at the registration desk she came into my room. Another nurse came in and gave me a tiny white pill to put under my tongue. Cee Cee brought a chair over to the bed and took my hand in hers. She never said a word. I felt as though her hand was my lifeline. I admit I was scared. I kept thinking about the kids and how they would react if they lost both parents within a week.

After a short while I felt myself begin to relax. "What's happening to me? Am I going to die?"

"No" she replied, "you are too stubborn for that. I don't know what is going on with you, but the Doctor will be in soon to talk to you. He is going over your test results now."

Just then Dr. Richards came into the room. "You gave us quite a scare tonight Lucy. There is no sign of any problems with your heart and all of your lab results have come back normal. How are you feeling?"

"Much calmer," I replied.

"I am pretty sure you had a panic attack from all of the stress you have been under the past few days."

"I thought I was having a heart attack."

"Panic attacks often feel that way. Are you sleeping?"

"Not very well."

"When was the last time you had something to eat?"

"Early this morning. I had a piece of toast before the

funeral."

"You know better than that," he admonished me. "I would like to keep you here for a couple more hours, and then we will repeat the ECG and blood tests. If there are no changes you can go home."

I began to protest but Cee Cee interrupted me, "She isn't going anywhere, I'll make sure of that."

"I am going to write you a prescription for anxiety medication. I want you to take these pills for a couple weeks and then we will re-evaluate and decide whether you should stay on them or not."

"No," I replied. "I don't want them.

He looked at Cee Cee and she shrugged her shoulders.

"Maybe you could try this if you feel this way again. Take five deep breaths and start counting backward from one hundred. The human brain can only focus on one thing at a time. If that doesn't work I want you back here, then we will take a second look at the medication."

"My brain doesn't work that way," I replied, "sometimes I feel like it never stops working/"

"You have a long difficult road ahead of you Lucy," he added. "You need to eat regularly and get as much rest as you can. Think of your children and grandchildren, they need you more than ever. You, falling apart isn't going to be good for any of you. I don't know if you are aware but there are support groups you can attend that may benefit you.

These people are going through the same trauma that you are."

"I don't need a support group. Besides Jim wouldn't like the idea of me telling strangers my feelings."

"I am only mentioning this because some of my other patients have found them very helpful"

I didn't want to hear any more, "Maybe I'll consider going later but not now. "I replied to placate him.

I stayed at the hospital for four more hours. The medication made me sleepy, but each time I opened my eyes Cee Cee was there beside me. Now, when I look back, I don't know how I would have coped without her.

. "Please don't tell my children about this," I begged her. "They don't need to have to worry about me too."

The second set of tests came back normal and Cee Cee took me home.

While I was dressing she said, "Maybe your doctor has the right idea. Talking will help."

I ignored her comment and wisely she didn't bring the subject up again.

After that, each time I felt anxious I did what Dr. Richards told me to do. I have no idea how it worked, but it did.

CHAPTER FOUR

Cee Cee must have said something to the kids because after that they took turns staying with me during the day. Not that I minded, I really didn't like being alone in the house. It felt too big for one person.

At night, when I couldn't sleep, I puttered. I divided the food people brought. Some I froze for myself and sent the rest home with the kids. Donnie took most of it – a confirmed bachelor, especially one who didn't know how to cook, had to eat.

I cleaned my house from top to bottom, except for our bedroom. Remembering was too difficult so I still slept on the couch, but never more than two or three hours at a time.

I forced myself to write thank you notes. The mail brought the usual utility bills and bank statements. I didn't know exactly what to do with them, so I let them pile up on the small table in the hallway. Jim always looked after paying the bills, and I was afraid to face the truth. I didn't know to whom or how to pay them and, if I started, that would be one more admission Jim was gone. *There will be time for that later.*

I missed Jim the most around supper time. He liked me to have supper ready when he came home from work. If he was late I made him a plate and put it into the fridge. When he got home I warmed it in the microwave while he washed up.

In the early years we would sit and talk – tell each other about our day. When the kids were growing up supper was usually hectic because we were in a hurry to get the children to their activities. Then after Jim joined the Investors Club he would gobble down his food, change his clothes and leave.

I resented him going out two or three evenings a week but kept telling myself, *this is good. He needs something outside of work that interests him.*

I was at loose ends. I didn't know what to do with myself. I started one thing after another and then forget what I was doing. I would walk into a room and forget why I was there. Without Jim I felt as though part of me was missing.

Each morning I told myself *all I have to do is get through today, nothing more, and nothing less.* The evenings were the longest. Cee Cee stopped by most days and, if not, she phoned. I kept the television on loud so there was some noise in the house. I even thought about getting a cat for company although I am allergic to cat hair.

I knew the kids, especially the girls, were concerned about me and I was careful not to let them know how I was feeling. In many ways Jim's passing was harder on them than on me because they were close to their dad. Kids today think their parents are going to live for ever

One day Donnie asked me," how come you never talk about dad, or mention his name?"

"I know I don't, but I think about him all the time."

I thought I had faced the worst life could throw at me so I wasn't prepared for that day my life irrevocably changed again. Angie and her kids spent the afternoon with me and had just left. I was tired and needed some time alone. That was when I grieved and tried to make some sort of sense out of all that had taken place in the last several weeks. Little did anybody realize I was hanging on by a thread.

I had just finished making a fresh pot of coffee when the doorbell rang. I hurried to the door and opened it. "What did you forget this time?" I blurted out, assuming it was Angie. Instead a stranger stood there.

"Lucille Barnes?" he asked.

"Yes," I answered him warily.

"You don't know me, but my name is Larry McAdams. I was a close friend of Jim's. May I come in?"

The man in front of me was slim, fine boned, of medium height, dressed in a white shirt, black pants and highly polished black shoes. In many ways he reminded me of a used car salesman.

"Oh yes, I recognize you. I saw you at the funeral." He was with one of the groups I didn't know. "I just made fresh coffee, would you care for some?"

"I would appreciate that," he replied. He took off his shoes at the door and placed them neatly side by side.

"Follow me and we will go into the kitchen. How did you know Jim?" I asked as we walked down the hallway.

He sat down on the edge of one of the chairs and appeared nervous. I poured us both a cup of coffee and put a plate of chocolate chip cookies on the table in front of us "Cream and sugar?"

"No, this is fine. Thank you." He sat quietly for several seconds and then uttered those fateful words.

"Mrs. Barnes, I don't know how to say this, so I will just come out with it. James and I were more than good friends, he was my husband. We had a commitment ceremony five years ago."

I felt myself sway and reached for the edge of the table. He jumped off his chair and helped me sit down.

"What did you just say?" I thought my ears were deceiving me.

"James was my husband" he repeated. "We were married five years ago. I brought the marriage certificate with me if you want to look at it?"

I took the official looking document and stared at it. I looked up at him and asked, "How can this be? Jim and I were married for twenty-five years."

"I know," he replied. "I am sorry to spring this on you. I wanted James to tell you, but he kept putting it off because didn't want to hurt you."

"I don't understand. How can this be possible?"

"This is different from a marriage certificate; rather it's a contract we signed between us. This contract is legally binding in all aspects."

I heard what he was saying but my mind refused to accept the implication that my husband was gay and in a relationship with another man.

"How did you meet Jim?" I asked. I felt as though I was talking through a tunnel.

"We met when he joined our Investors group."

Suddenly I felt sick. I was the one who encouraged Jim to join that group and attend the meetings. He was always interested in money and learning how to make money work for him.

"Mrs. Barnes, James was confused about his sexuality. He loved you and his children, but he loved me too."

I didn't want to hear any more. I stood up so suddenly that the chair fell over backwards. "Get out," I screamed at him. "How dare you sit there and tell me these lies? I don't believe you."

"Mrs. Barnes," he replied gently. "I am telling you the truth. I'm sorry I have to be the one to tell you."

"Why are you here? What do you want?" I challenged him. "Don't try and tell me you came out of the goodness of your heart, to console the grieving widow?"

"No. Actually I need a copy of the death certificate. Like you, I have financial matters that need to be taken care of."

"I will be hiring Brian Sanderson as my lawyer, you can

talk to him." Suddenly I was crying,

"I need you to leave now." I shrieked desperately trying to hold my emotions together.

He got off the chair, walked down the hall way to the front door then bent down to put on his shoes. When he stood up I saw tears running down his face. He took a tissue from the box sitting on the corner of the hallway table and dabbed his eyes.

"Mrs. Barnes, James was a good man. I loved him, and I don't know how to go on without him."

"I know," I replied, "that makes two of us."

I stood at the door and watched him walk to his car. His shoulders were rounded and his steps were slow. When he got to his car he turned and waved. I stood there for a long time watching until his taillights disappeared. When I walked into the living room, I picked up one of the many vases filled with flowers and threw it against the wall.

I screamed at Jim, "all these years and I never suspected. You should have told me. How could you do this to me and your children? I hate you."

I called him every name I could think of. One after another I threw the vases at the wall. Water ran down and seeped into the carpet, flowers were heaped in a colorful pile. I screamed and screamed at him until I collapsed on the floor, curled up into a fetal position and cried all the tears I had been holding back.

"Why?" I sobbed. "Why wasn't I enough?"

CHAPTER FIVE

Sometime during the night I must have moved from the floor to the couch because I woke up shivering in spite of the afghan wrapped around my shoulders. My eyes were sore from the tears I shed the night before. The insistent ringing of the doorbell and the sound of somebody pounding on the front door must have been what woke me up. I ran my fingers through my hair and stumbled over the upended coffee table to see who was there. I noticed I was wearing the same clothes as the day before.

As soon as I opened the door Donnie pushed his way inside. "Why didn't you answer your phone," he demanded." I drove over to make sure you were okay."

"I didn't hear the phone ring. What time is it any way?"

"Ten o'clock in the morning."

"Oh." I wondered how long I slept.

He pushed his way past me and walked into the living room. "Mom, what in God's name went on here last night?"

The living room was a shambles, broken glass and flowers all over the floor, and water stains running down the wall. The coffee table was overturned and a broken lamp lay inside the door.

"I don't know," I answered. *Oh Lord, how am I going to*

explain this as well as tell him and his sisters that their dad was gay?

"Oh mom," he said, folding me into his arms. "We'll get through this. You'll see. Now do you want to tell me what happened here?" He asked, gesturing to the chaos surrounding us.

"No," I replied, resting my head on his shoulder.

He held me for a long time. "You look like crap, why don't you go upstairs, have a shower and I'll clean this mess up."

When I came back downstairs I smelled fresh coffee. The flowers had been picked up and the broken glass vacuumed from the carpet. The coffee table was in its usual place, and he must have thrown the lamp into the garbage.

I heard him talking on his phone. "You should have seen this place when I walked in. It looked like a tornado had passed through here." He listened for a bit and then replied, "No, she is fine. I am going to stay for a while and will call you later."

"Who were you talking to?" I asked.

"Amy," he replied.

"Did you have to call and alarm her? I have everything under control whether you believe it or not." I poured myself a cup of coffee, sat down on my usual chair and stared out the window.

He must have noticed the two cups in the sink. "Was

somebody here last night?"

"A friend of your dad's stopped by."

"What did he want? Angie told me it was well after seven before she left. Why would somebody stop by to visit so late?"

"I don't want to talk about it," I replied.

"What in the hell went on here last night?" he exploded. "The last thing I expected was to walk into something like this. Mom, talk to me, what is going on?"

"I have already told you, I don't want to talk about it," I snapped back at him, "now let it go."

When I saw the look on his face I apologized. "I'm sorry. I didn't mean to yell at you. I have to figure some things out first before I can explain what happened and why."

Then I added, "Donnie would you phone Brian Sanderson's office and make an appointment for me? Whether I want to or not, there are a few things I need to take care of."

"Did dad have a will?"

"Yes, but it is fifteen years old. We both do, and they are at Brian's office."

Donnie pulled his cell phone from his shirt pocket, turned and walked down the hall way. I heard him talking.

As I sat there things suddenly started to make sense. The

many nights Jim was working late, the weekend fishing trips at the cabin with the "boys," and the fact that he hadn't made love to me for five years. Like a puzzle all of the pieces began to fall in place.

I felt nauseated and dizzy. *How could I have been so clueless? So many times I felt I should have talked to him about how much he had changed, but I couldn't. Maybe I didn't want to know?*

Donnie called out to me. "Mom, I can get an appointment for three this afternoon, is that good for you."

"Yes." I replied.

I heard him say a little more into his phone, and then he came back into the kitchen. "When was the last time you ate something?" he asked.

"When Angie and the kids were here, but I don't seem to be hungry these days."

"How about I make you some cinnamon toast like you used to do for us?"

When the kids weren't feeling well or hurt, I made them cinnamon toast. That was my magic cure for everything. I didn't feel like eating, but I agreed anyway.

"Do you remember the first time you decided to make it for yourselves?"

He nodded his head. "If I remember correctly there was more cinnamon and sugar on the floor than on our toast."

While we ate, we chatted a bit about his job as a Parts man at a local heavy equipment dealership, and about Angie and Amy's children.

"Are you going to be okay if I leave you alone for a while?" he asked. "I have to check in at the shop, but I'll be back in time to take you to Brian's office."

"I will be fine," I assured him. "Go and do what you have to. Life goes on Donnie, and we have no choice but to go along with it."

I sat and finished my coffee and absently mindedly put our cups and plates into the dish washer. I went back to the living room, lay down and pulled the blanket up to my chin.

Take this one step at a time Lucy, and see how it plays out. I wish this was all a nightmare and when I woke up, life would be normal again, but I know it's not going to happen.

CHAPTER SIX

When Donnie and I arrived at Brian's office he was waiting for us. "Please come in and have a chair," he said. "Can I get you something to drink?" We both shook our heads no.

His office was as neat as a pin. Along one wall was a bookshelf, all the books the same size and color coded. On the other side of the room there was a credenza with files on top and tray with a carafe of ice water and several glasses. On top of the large mahogany desk he had a picture of his wife and children, a lap top and two file folders. The walls were empty except for his framed law degree.

Donnie and I sat side by side on two black chairs facing Brian's desk. I could see Donnie was tense so I reached over and squeezed his hand.

"I am sorry to hear about your loss." Brian began. "I liked Jim, he was a good man. I had my secretary go into your file and bring me Jim's will. This one is dated fifteen years ago, is there any chance there is one more current?"

"Not that I know of," I replied. "We had those made up when we went on a holiday to Mexico. If something happened to us we wanted to be sure the kids would be taken care of."

Brian paused and read the document carefully. "I don't see any problems. I will have my secretary put the advertisement in next week's paper with a date of a month from now."

"Advertisement, what for?" I asked.

"I guess I should explain more clearly. The first thing we have to do is see if there are any outside claims on the estate. We need to find out who Jim might have owed money to. In the meantime I will file for his death benefits, but for his insurance and other benefits I will need the original documents."

I looked at him. "I have no idea what you are talking about. Jim looked after all of that."

Donne looked at me "Mom, are you serious? Didn't you and dad ever talk about these things?"

"We never talked about a lot of things. He looked after our business affairs and finances. Each month he put so much into a bank account for household expenses. That's the way he wanted it."

"I guess we'll have to start looking then. Do you know where he kept all of his important papers?" Donnie asked.

"They are probably locked in his desk drawer at home."

"But the utility bills, and the bank statements that came in the mail, didn't you open them?"

"No. If the mail was addressed to your dad I wasn't allowed to open it." I answered.

The two men looked at each other. "We have to get that information mom. Do you have a key to dad's desk?"

"I think so, but I'll have to look and see if I can find it." A chill passed over me. "Is something wrong?'

"Oh no Mrs. Barnes," Brian quickly said. "It's just a little unusual that's all, usually it's the other way around. The wife looks after all the details in a home, and the husband doesn't have a clue. But don't worry, we will figure everything out."

I looked at Donnie and then at Brian. "Is that everything you need for today? I have a terrible headache. I can't seem to concentrate these days."

"Understandably so," Brian said, and then he turned to Donnie "Can I count on you to help your mom find what we need. This is a daunting task at the best of times. I will get my secretary started on some of the necessary paper work today."

The two men shook hands and then Brian said, "Donnie, I would like to speak to your mom alone for a minute. Do you mind?"

Donnie got a funny look on his face. "I'll wait outside for you mom," he replied and left the room.

Once the door closed Brian asked me, "do you know a man by the name of Larry McAdams?'

"I have met him, yes."

"He called me this morning, asked for a copy of Jim's

death certificate and if he could stop by to bring me a copy of Jim's Will. He made it sound like he had a newer one than what we have."

"He didn't waste much time," I muttered. "Last evening he stopped by the house and I told him if he wanted any information he should talk to you. I didn't mean to put you in a difficult situation. I didn't think he would be in such a hurry and I would have time to see you first."

"Mrs. Barnes, you are my client, not him. Is there anything I need to know before I meet with him?"

"I can't tell you," I whispered. Tears filled my eyes. "Please don't mention this to Donnie or the girls until we find out what he wants."

"Mrs. Barnes, there is such a thing as lawyer client confidentiality. I can't repeat anything you tell me not even to your children without your permission."

"I know, and I will share more information with you, but not today."

"What do you want me to do about Mr. McAdams' request?"

"Nothing for now if that is possible?"

As he opened the door he smiled and said, "You're the boss. Thank you for coming Mrs. Barnes. I will need those documents from you as soon as possible." Donnie was sitting in a chair waiting for me.

"I understand, but I have no idea where to start looking."

I replied.

He must have recognized the dazed look on my face. "Joan, please get one of those Estate packages for Mrs. Barnes?" he said to his receptionist.

Handing it to me, he added "all the information you need is in here. If you aren't sure or have any questions don't hesitate to call."

When we got to his truck Donnie turned to me and asked, "What did he want to talk to you about?"

"He wanted to explain lawyer client confidentiality."

"Why couldn't he do that when I was in the room?'

"I am not sure," I replied. *Oh Donnie, please don't ask me anymore, at least until I find out what Larry McAdams wants. I need to think this through before I tell you and your sisters that your dad was gay, and our whole life was a sham.*

Donnie dropped me off in the driveway. I went inside the house, put my purse on the hall table and stumbled over to the couch. All I wanted to do was sleep. When I sleeping, I didn't have to come up with the answers to all of the questions I knew were to come.

CHAPTER SEVEN

Several days after my visit to Brian's office, Amy came to see me. "I think it is time for you to move upstairs and start sleeping in your bed," she declared. "You are not resting properly and dad wouldn't want you to do this."

"I can't. I'm not ready." I replied.

"Not ready for what mom?"

"All of his things are still in there. I smell his aftershave every time I walk into the room. The paraphernalia from the ambulance is still all over the floor and I can still see him lying there. I…."

"Mom dad is dead, and nothing is going to change that. At some point you are going to have to deal with this."

"What if I don't want to?" I snapped at her. "You kids need to leave me alone, and I will do what I have to when I am ready, and not before."

She got a funny look on her face but didn't back down. In many ways she was just as stubborn as her dad.

"I'm sorry Amy," I apologized, "I know your heart is in the right place, and you are right."

"How about if Angie and I come over tomorrow and help you clean up your room? Maybe, once you have a chance to think this over, you will change your mind. When we get here you can always tell us to leave if you want to."

"Fair enough," I agreed.

After she left I went up to our bedroom. Other than grabbing clean clothes I avoided spending any time in there. I noticed that someone had cleaned up the mess on the floor left by the paramedics and made the bed.

I don't know what I expected. I still smelled Jim's unique musky scent of aftershave and diesel fuel. I could feel his presence. I thought of the many nights I wanted him to hold me, to make love to me but he turned away and lay on his side, his back toward me.

His watch and a few coins lay on his night stand. The clothes he had taken off that night when he came to bed were still crumpled in front of the laundry hamper. Even after twenty-five years I hadn't been able to convince him to lift the hamper lid and put them inside. Automatically I picked up his dirty clothes and put them inside the hamper just as I used to do every other morning.

Even though everything was the same, the room felt different. I had slept beside him for twenty-five years but didn't know who he was. I had no idea what his thoughts were and what secrets he kept from me.

"Did you ever love me?" I screamed into the stillness of the room, then turned and left.

I thought I heard him answer me, "Yes I did Lucy, but not in the way you deserved to be loved. Please forgive me. I never meant to hurt you. You deserved so much more than I was able to give you. Go now and be happy."

The girls are right. It is time.

* * *

The next morning, when the girls arrived, I was waiting for them. They brought several empty cardboard boxes and a package of green garbage bags. Amy carried the biggest bottle of Baileys Irish Cream I have ever seen in one hand and a cardboard tray with three large cups of coffee in her other.

"In case we need some fortification," she stated before I had a chance to say anything.

Before we went upstairs she topped the cups of coffee off with the liqueur. "Here's to you mom." She said holding up her cup Angie and I joined her.

"We don't want to push you mom. Tell us what you want. I thought we could donate dad's clothes to the men's shelter downtown, keep what you want and then decide what to do with the rest later. If we aren't sure, we could put the article on the bed."

"I wonder if Donnie will want any of this," I remarked.

"I asked him, he said to let it all go." Angie said.

Taking a deep breath I walked into our bedroom, over to the dresser and opened his top drawer. Our dresser had six drawers, three for me and three for him. This was the easy part. The drawers held his underwear, socks, T-shirts and they went into a bag for the men's shelter.

The closet was a different story. Jim hated to throw things away. In fact he still had his leather jacket from high school tucked in the back. Each time I suggested he toss it away I was informed "it still fits." Which of course it didn't and hadn't for a long time.

"I don't know why he kept this? I don't think anybody would want it now." I remarked as I placed it on the bed.

One item at a time we made decisions. Some brought tears to my eyes, memories of days long past. Others went straight into the garbage bags. I didn't know whether to laugh or cry, but the Baileys and coffee must have helped because we drank most of the bottle. Actually, the process wasn't as hard as I thought it would be.

When I opened the drawer of his nightstand table the first thing I saw was the key to his desk. For a minute I thought my heart stopped.

"What have you got there?" Angie asked.

"The key to your father's desk, I was wondering where it was."

"Good, we can check that out while we're here."

"No, I will do it later. There are some important papers Brian wants me to look for."

Angie took a bag of clothes downstairs. "How are you doing Mom?" Amy asked. I could see the concern written over her face.

"Better than I expected. It was good having you girls help me. I was dreading this task."

"Do you think you will be able to sleep in here tonight?"

"I'm not sure, but I will try."

I helped the girls carry the rest of the bags and boxes downstairs. "Now that we've started this we might as well finish. I'll get Donnie to come over and help me with the garage."

When they were ready to leave I hugged each of them. "Thank you. I couldn't have done this without you."

That night I crawled into my bed, wrapped my arms around Jim's pillow and cried myself to sleep. In one way I felt a sense of accomplishment, but in another, I felt today was one more way I was saying goodbye to the years we shared together.

CHAPTER EIGHT

Slowly I adapted to the fact that Jim was gone and I was alone. I knew there was more I had to deal with, and the secret I was keeping from my children. I realized life goes on, and each of us has a choice as to whether we participate or not.

Jim made me feel like I needed to be looked after and not capable of making my own decisions. When I think back he rarely asked my opinion and did most of the decision making for us. Outside of being involved with the children's activities I kept to myself.

One thing I refuse to do is allow Larry McAdams to walk all over me, and to accept that he played a bigger role in Jim's life the last five years than I did, or that he made Jim happy when I couldn't.

Two weeks after Donnie and I were at Brian Sanderson's phoned and I was forced out of the safe little bubble I wrapped around myself.

"Mrs. Barnes, have you had time to go through Jim's papers yet?" he asked.

"No. I keep putting it off. Why?"

"We need to find out if there are any insurance policies on the house or the cabin, or if Jim had any life insurance. I don't want to push you, but I need this information."

After hanging up the phone, I went into our bedroom, and took Jim's desk key out of the drawer of his nightstand. For some reason I was reluctant to go through Jim's desk. Maybe I was afraid of what I would find. Even now I felt like an intruder as I entered Jim's office. This was always his private domain that I was not allowed to enter. *What I don't know can't hurt me. I sure hope there are no surprises waiting for me.*

The office was well organized. All of his files were in the four drawer filing cabinet and up to date. It was easy to find most of the documents I needed. That left only the desk and his lap top to be searched, but I didn't know his password. I was barely computer literate so that didn't intimidate me.

The first drawer I opened contained pens, pencils, job descriptions from work – nothing I deemed important. I tossed most if it into the garbage can beside his desk. I used the key to unlock the top drawer and the first thing I saw was an intimate photo of him and Larry McAdams taken at the cabin. There was a marriage agreement signed by both of them, and bank statements with Jim's name on them, but with a different address.

I dumped the drawer on top of the desk, and went through each piece of paper one at a time.

There was a life insurance policy for one hundred thousand dollars with Larry McAdams was the beneficiary. I found bank statements which showed that Jim borrowed a large amount of money, using our house as collateral. There was a copy of a purchase agreement for a new car and credit card statements owing thousands of dollars.

I was in shock. *The man I knew was careful with his money. He didn't spend recklessly and thought twice before making a large purchase. Where is the title to our house and to our cabin at Rochester Lake? Where is the money he said he was putting away for our retirement? What are these bills for furniture and art supplies? Did he hate me so much that he felt he needed to keep all of this a secret from me? I am confused. None of this is making any sense.*

I gathered everything I found and put it into a large brown envelope then phoned Brian's office to make an appointment.

The next morning, as soon as his office opened, I was waiting. I handed him the envelope containing the papers I found in Jim's desk.

He looked them over, and then looked at me. "Did you know about any of this?"

"No, I had no idea. Jim and I didn't talk much about money."

"Mrs. Barnes, I don't know how to tell you this but Jim was broke. He remortgaged your house and hadn't made any payments for the last three months. He stopped paying for your health insurance over a year ago, and yesterday I received a bill from the hospital for eight thousand dollars. The bill for the funeral home has also arrived and it is nearly five thousand dollars."

"This doesn't make any sense. I thought our health insurance was paid from work?"

"No, he withdrew from that and cashed out all the retirement funds he accumulated. Then there is Larry McAdams claim."

"What about him?" I asked

"He brought in a signed notarized will Jim made three years ago that leaves everything to him, particularly the new house Jim bought and the cabin at the lake. The new car they bought was insured naming him as the beneficiary. Unfortunately, this leaves you responsible for all of the credit card debts, the late house payments, the hospital and funeral costs plus the other small debts that are trickling in."

I couldn't believe what I was hearing. I looked at him and asked. "How can this be possible?"

"I am sorry to be the bearer of such bad news and I don't know what to tell you."

"If I am going to have to pay for all of this, I .don't know how I can? I don't even know how I am going to live for the next few months. In fact, I'm not sure how I am going to pay you." I shouldn't have been surprised. As soon as Larry McAdams showed up I had a feeling there would be trouble.

"Do you have any money at all?" Brian asked.

"Only his last pay cheque. Does that have to go into his estate too?"

He nodded his head yes.

I felt sick to my stomach. I didn't want to ask the next question but knew I had to. "The one thing I have is my house. Does this mean I am going to have to sell it to cover these debts?"

"I am afraid so, that would be my suggestion. I don't see any other way around this and I can't close your file until everything is taken care of. If you get a good price, there may be some left for you. I don't know if I mentioned this before, you will receive a small monthly survivor's pension from the government which is outside of the estate. As for my fee we will arrange for it to be paid by the estate."

"I understand, but how am I going to explain this to Donnie and the girls?"

"We could do it here at the office. That way there will be only one explanation rather than having to explain three times."

I thought for a moment. *Perhaps a professional setting would be better than being at home. They will be angry but will control themselves here. At home it would be nothing but a free for all. Barnes tempers run hot at the best of times.*

After thinking over his suggestion for several minutes I replied "I think that's a good idea

"Mrs. Barnes I am so sorry this is happening to you. Let me know when you are ready."

"I am too Brian," I replied. "This mess is partly my fault. I should have paid more attention to things, and asked more questions, but I trusted Jim to look after us. It appears too much so."

By the time I got home I was nearly hysterical. I phoned Cee Cee immediately.

"Hi Lucy, I was wondering if you would call. How did you make out at the Lawyer's today?"

I couldn't answer her.

"Lucy, are you there? What's wrong? Talk to me."

"Can you come over?" I managed to get past the huge lump in my throat. "I need someone to talk to."

"I'll be there in ten minutes. I'm on my way.

When she came through the door, I threw my arms around her as though she was a life preserver in a raging sea. I stood in the comfort of her arms and cried deep gulping sobs.

When I stopped she led me into the kitchen and made a fresh pot of coffee. I sat there staring out the window for a long time and she didn't push me to talk. When the coffee was finished she poured both of us a cup.

"Are you ready to tell me why you are so worked up?"

"I have to sell my house."

"What? You better start at the beginning and tell me what this is about."

I told her everything – how I found out Jim was gay and committed to a man; that he left everything to Larry and left me with a pile of bills. At least with her I could be nakedly honest.

When I finished she looked at me, "Did you have any idea?"

"No Jim handled our personal finances and put so much money into a bank account for me every month for household expenses. Right after we were married he started this because he didn't think I would be responsible enough with his money. He used to say, "I make it and I will decide how we spend it. I guess I just got used to it. I honestly thought that was how most married people handled their finances. I learned later that his dad did the same thing with his mother."

"Is there anything left for you?"

The furniture and whatever is left after I sell the house and pay off the debts."

"Do you think you could appeal to this Larry guy for help? He must realize the position Jim left you and the children?"

"No way in hell. We both know where Jim's priorities lay and they certainly weren't at home." I replied sarcastically.

"Have you told your kids any of this yet?"

"No not yet. How do I say to them, "by the way, your dad was gay and left everything to his gay lover? Oh, and not only that, he left me with a mountain of bills and I am going to have to sell the house to pay them. He didn't think enough of us to make sure we were provided for. How would you do it?"

"I don't know honey. I wouldn't want to be in your shoes."

"I don't know if I can do this to them. I will be destroying everything they thought and loved about their dad."

"I know," she replied. We sat there quietly for a long time, each lost in her thoughts.

Breaking the silence she asked, "What are you going to do after all of this is over?"

"I guess I'll have to try and find a job, but I have never worked outside the house and I'm not trained for anything. I haven't thought that far ahead yet."

"You have to tell your children Lucy. You can't keep this from them much longer."

"I know and I will. Brian Sanderson suggested we all meet in his office."

"That's a good idea. When?"

I started to cry again. "Cee Cee what am I going to do?"

"I don't know but I do know one thing about you Lucy and that is you are a survivor. You will find a way."

Then she looked at me and asked," how do you really feel about all of this? I know you are keeping a lot inside."

"I don't know if I can find the right words. I am beyond angry. I feel abused and humiliated. Jim let on that we had this perfect marriage when he knew differently. Did everybody know about Jim except me? Mostly though, I feel used. I cooked for him, raised his children and bent over backwards to please him for twenty-five years and for what?" By this time I was screeching at her

"Lucy you need to stop."

"No I don't. You asked me how I felt and I am telling you. I am left with nothing except memories that are lies and pile of bills to pay. Cee Cee, the fact is he loved Larry McAdams and I was merely a convenience."

"I don't know what to say…."

I laughed bitterly. "There is nothing to say. He died and now I will never know – did he love me or not?"

"Lucy you still have your children to love and support you. They need you now more than ever."

I began to calm down. "At least he got that right. How did this happen? Why didn't I see?"

"I would say first of all, that you loved and trusted him, and secondly, in his own way, Jim did love you. He wanted what the two of you had together and built over the years. I don't think he ever acknowledged the fact he was gay until Larry McAdams came into his life."

I looked at her. "It would have been better if he had been honest and upfront when his affair started."

"You are absolutely right," she agreed, "but it's too late for that now."

Cee Cee stayed for the rest of the evening. At some point I must have fallen asleep because I remember her covering me with a blanket, and kissing me on the forehead. "I'm going home now Lucy, are you going to be okay? Call me if you need anything."

Later, she told me she was afraid to leave me alone. She was worried I might do something to hurt myself. That thought never crossed my mind.

"I am fine," I replied half asleep. Sleep was a comfort for me – a hiding place when I didn't have to deal with what was happening around me.

The next morning I phoned her to let her know I was ready to set up an appointment with Brian. I let the answering machine take all of my calls. I had the television on, but the sound was muted. Except for having to go to the bathroom and finding something to eat, I stayed in bed for the next three days. There I was safe, nothing could hurt me.

On the morning of the fourth day I phoned Brian and set up an appointment for the next day. *I realized this problem is not going to go away and needed to be dealt with.* Brian told me he would call my children and ask them to come to his office so I wouldn't have to deal with this.

When I phoned Cee Cee she asked, "Do you want me to come over?" she asked

"No, but thanks anyway, I want to be alone."

"Do you want me to go with you to Brian's office?"

"No, but you could drive me if you like, and wait for me."

"You can do this Lucy," she stated.

"Cee Cee, what are our friends going to say when they find out. I can hear them already."

"The hell with them," she exploded. "That bastard didn't need to do this to you on top of everything else."

"You mean like dying?"

"You know exactly what I mean," she replied. Cee Cee had never liked Jim and tolerated him for my sake.

"Cee Cee getting mad isn't going to help. What's done is done."

"I guess you are right," she replied. "He never did have any consideration for you why would that change when he died?"

I didn't have an answer for her.

CHAPTER NINE

Brian arranged an appointment for us the following afternoon. I arrived early and was waiting in his office when the three of them arrived together.

"What is going on mom?" Donnie asked. "Why are we meeting here? I had to rearrange my schedule to be here." Amy and Angie were quiet. They were waiting for me to answer him.

To tell you the truth I would have rather been any place else but there. I knew how upset and angry my kids were going to be. *They have to be told at some point so today is as good a day as any.*

Once we were all seated around a long dark mahogany table in a small conference room Brian took over. "I asked you all to come here to discuss what is happening with your father's estate. There are some things you need to be aware of. Unfortunately, there is no easy way to do this. Your mother and I decided to get you together, so we only have to explain once."

They looked at each other with puzzled expressions and then to me for reassurance. I couldn't look at them.

"Your dad was deeply in debt when he died and, in order to settle the estate, your mom is going to have to sell the house."

Donnie was the first to speak. "How can that be?" he shouted. "He had a good job, worked hard all his life. I don't understand."

Brian looked at me and then continued. "Your dad left the bulk of his estate to a man by the name of Larry McAdams. He had borrowed heavily against the house and left behind thousands of dollars in credit card debt."

"Mom," Donnie continued to shout, "Who the hell is this Larry McAdams? I have never heard that name before. Who is this guy, and what did he have to do with dad?'

Then he turned to Brian, "what about the cabin? What did he do with that?"

Brian turned to me, "Mrs. Barnes, I think it is best if you tell them."

I saw how upset Donnie was getting, so I closed my eyes and blurted out the words. "Your dad was gay and Larry McAdams was his lover." Helplessly I looked at them "I didn't know," I whispered.

I breathed a sigh of relief. *There I have told them and finally they know the truth.*

The room was silent and then Amy began to cry. Donnie stood up and began pacing back and forth, muttering a litany of curse words. Then they all began shouting at me at the same time.

"How long have you known? Why didn't you tell us?

How could you have let him do this to us?"

My insides clenched and for a moment I thought I was going to be sick.

Finally Brian spoke up. "That's enough. Show your mother some respect. Unfortunately the person who should be explaining this situation is no longer with us." The shouting stopped.

"Did dad give him the cabin too?" Angie asked. The cabin was a special place for us. The kids and I used to stay there every summer during the holidays. My grandfather built the cabin on Rochester Lake and when I was a kid my mom and dad spent every summer there. Jim and I carried on the tradition with our children,

"Yes, everything except the boat and the motor."

"How much money are we talking about?" Donnie asked. He had finally sat down and stopped cursing.

"A little over two hundred and fifty thousand dollars, including what is still owed on the house. He remortgaged that last year." Brian answered

"Is there any insurance," Amy asked. "It's not like dad not to have everything covered."

"Not on your home, but the property he owned with Larry McAdams was fully insured."

Donnie looked at me, "I don't understand any of this. How could you let him do this to us?"

"Donnie, I didn't let your dad do this to us. I had no idea what he was doing. If I had, I would have tried to stop him."

Donnie began yelling at me again. "You have to fix this. You can't let dad give away what should have been ours."

Once again, Brian spoke up "Stop shouting Donnie. Blaming your mom isn't going to help. You can take this to court but I guarantee you will lose. The Will Larry McAdams showed me is legal and binding and supersedes the one I have.

Just so you know your mom is responsible for the credit card debt, the mortgage on the house, the medical and funeral bills as well as all of the other small amounts that are trickling in. I am waiting for the exact figures from the bank concerning the house but it looks like he was three months behind on his payments."

"What about the investments from the Investment Club he belonged to? Is there anything there we can cash out?" Donnie asked.

"There are no investments and there never was. You dad used that as an excuse to get out of the house."

I had a headache when I arrived at Brian's office, but now it was a thousand times worse. I felt nauseated, my vision was blurry and I felt as though my head was going to explode.

I stood up. "I have to go," I announced. "I can't stay here any longer."

"Do you need someone to drive you home Mrs. Barnes?"

"No. I have a ride, my friend Cee Cee is waiting for me downstairs."

"Mom, we will stop by after we leave here." Amy said.

"No. not today," I told them. "I need to be alone. Cee Cee will look after me. Come tomorrow when I can think more clearly."

As I was leaving I heard Brian say, "have the courtesy to give your mom some time and space. This whole situation has been a complete shock to her too."

Cee Cee was parked in front of the building. I got into her car, buckled up my seat belt and then leaned my head back.

"How did it go?" she asked.

"Like I thought it would. Donnie is still arguing the facts of which Will has to be followed.

They blame me," I replied.

"Oh honey, no they don't. They are in shock."

"I know, but their world just tumbled down, and the memories of their father will be changed forever."

"The one fact that won't change is how much he loved them." She replied, reaching over and patting my knee.

"You and I know that, but how do I convince them?"

Cee Cee dropped me off in the driveway. She must have sensed I wanted to be alone. When I got into the house I took two Tylenol and went straight to bed. Everything I thought was true about my life was a lie. I was finished crying over Jim. He made his choices and I hadn't even come out in second place.

Never again am I going to trust a man. I will never give another person that much control over me again.

CHAPTER TEN

The next morning I got up earlier than usual, put on a pot of coffee and waited. I knew the kids would be upset when they left Brian's office yesterday, and would be here first thing in the morning.

Jim how could you leave me this mess to clean up? What on earth were you thinking? You should have been honest with me instead of trying to juggle two different worlds. I don't know how I am going to do this. I also don't know why I thought talking to a dead man was going to help, but I seemed to be doing that a lot lately.

I didn't have to wait long. By eight o'clock the girls arrived, their eyes red from crying and lack of sleep. Donnie arrived about ten minutes later.

"Coffee is ready," I announced, walking back into the kitchen. "You both look like you could use some." I sat down on my usual chair; they filled their cups and sat on either side of me.

"Mom" I heard Donnie call out.

"In the kitchen...."

Amy got up, poured him a cup of coffee and put it on the table. He came in and sat across the table from me. Nobody said a word, and then Angie started to cry.

"That's not going to help," Donnie snapped at her. She began to cry harder.

Suddenly their pent up rage boiled over. "Leave her alone," Amy screamed at him.

. The fight was on, just like when they were younger. The girls always stood together against Donnie.

I let them go for a few minutes, and then yelled loud enough for them to hear me. "That's enough. How old are you? I thought I would be dealing with adults today."

"Amy looked at me. "Mom how could he do this to us?"

I lost it on them. "Do what to you? No matter his sexual orientation, your dad was always there for you. He was proud of you and your accomplishments. He drove you wherever you needed to go." I looked at Donnie, "he never missed a hockey game. He did everything a dad was supposed to do and then some. Besides, he didn't do anything to you, he did it to me.

You have your jobs, your homes and your families. I understand why you are hurt and angry. I feel exactly the same way, but that doesn't change the facts. I still have to come up with two hundred and fifty thousand dollars to pay his bills and that means I have to sell the house to do it."

"Did you know he was gay mom?" Angie asked.

"No, not until Larry McBride came to see me a couple of days after the funeral."

"Did you still have sex with him?" Donnie asked.

38

"No not for the last five years."

"Maybe that should have been your first clue. You didn't wonder what was wrong?" he replied sarcastically.

I wasn't going to discuss my sex life with my children. "Sometimes," I answered truthfully.

"Mom, "Angie wailed "how could he give that man everything that the two of you worked for? It's not fair that there is nothing left for us."

"That's not true," I answered her. "We still have lots of good memories."

"I guess he loved him more than us," Amy commented.

"It appears that way," I replied.

I didn't want them to see how broken and hurt I was. I wanted them to remember their dad as he was, not be defined by what they learned at the end. I guess a mother's instinct is to try and protect her children, no matter how old they are.

I looked over at Donnie and tears were running down his face. "He was a good man, and a good dad and he loved you. That is all you need to remember." I continued.

Amy got up, refilled our coffee cups and sat down again.

"I need your help," I told them. "I don't know how to do any of the things I am expected to do now."

I probably could have muddled my way through but I

wanted them to be part of the process. I thought that by helping me make decisions they would begin to heal.

"Have you given any thought to what you are going to do after you sell the house?" Angie asked.

"I've thought about that a lot. I'm going to find a small apartment I can afford and find a job. You kids can take whatever you want from the house, and I will keep enough to furnish a new place. The rest we will sell, or burn, or whatever you decide to do. Any money that we make has to be turned into Brian to pay the estate bills. There is a small survivor benefit from the government for me to live on, but I don't know how much it will be. Brian is working on that."

"Do you think there will be any left for you?"

"I have no idea. I guess it depends on how much we get for the house." The kids looked at me.

"Are you going to be okay mom," Donnie asked. By now he was much calmer.

"Someday, but not right now," I answered. I think for the first time they realized how truly devastated I was.

Angie spoke up. "Let's come back on Saturday and we can begin to sort things out. In the meantime mom can decide what she wants to keep, and we can decide what we would like to have. I'll look into what is available for apartments and how much the rents are. Donnie, you have a friend who is a real estate agent, maybe you could talk to her and get an idea of what we can get for the house.

She turned and looked at me, "We got this mom. You don't need to worry about a thing."

"Thank you," I whispered.

Donnie was the last to leave. "I can't believe that Larry guy isn't offering to help you in some way. I feel like finding him and punching him in the face."

"That won't accomplish anything, besides I wouldn't accept his help even if he offered. He is aware of the situation, and will have to live with his conscience. As much as we wish to change what has happened we can't. All we can do is find a way that will help us move on from here."

"You are a bigger person that I am mom, I can't be like you."

CHAPTER ELEVEN

When Saturday rolled around I was mentally prepared for a hard day. Instead it turned out to be the best day we had as a family, since Jim died. I was also able to make some decisions about what needed to be done.

Angie, Amy and Donnie were there by ten. The girls looked tired but their mood changed when Donnie came in with a case of cold beer.

"What?" he said as he walked in, "if dad was here he would have a cold one with us."

"You remind me of him when you say that. He always said a cold one fixes everything, even at ten o'clock in the morning. We might as well get started," I suggested.

"Have each of you decided what you want of your dad's? If you come across something you gave him and want to keep it, put it into the box on the dining room table with your name on it." Grinning I added "and no fighting."

Donnie chose Jim's fishing tackle and golf clubs. Amy asked for his lounge chair. Angie was a little more hesitant. "It's okay honey, take your time. You don't have to decide today. If you want a memento for your children feel free to take it.

"Mom," Donnie said, "in three weeks there is an estate and household auction sale at the Auction Barn. Apparently dad was a frequent customer and, when I called yesterday, the manager said he would be glad to include your items."

I laughed. "Going to auctions was one of your dads favorite past times. You wouldn't believe some of the junk he brought home and then wonder why he bought it in the first place."

"Sounds like a good idea to me," I answered him but my mind was screaming *it's too soon,*

Donnie and I went to the garden shed in the backyard. The girls began in the house. There wasn't much of value in the shed except two lawnmowers, one of which didn't work. I remember Jim always meant to fix and sell it, but he never did. Most of what was in there was junk so we piled it into the back of Donnie's truck and he made the first of many trips to the dump.

I left Donnie outside and when I went into the kitchen to help the girls they weren't sure what to do. The cupboard doors were open, and a few bowls say on the kitchen table. I looked at them and it was all I could do to keep from screaming.

"Slow pokes," I chided them, "we have already finished the shed."

"We didn't know where to start or what you want to keep," Angie stated.

"Then, I guess the first step is to figure out what I can take with me when I find an apartment. I will put the more personal items we can't decide upon in storage for now and we can sort them out later. Donnie is going to start in the garage. I don't know what half of it is or what it's used for."

Several hours later my two son-in-law's arrived with my grandchildren and a large bag of groceries.

"We brought steak and salad fixings," Warren, Amy's husband announced. "Show me to the barbecue." Looking at Amy he said, "Woman you are in charge of the salad, Angie can take care of the potatoes."

There was laughter in the air. The doom and gloom evaporated and suddenly the day took on new meaning. These were the kind of days Jim enjoyed the most.

The girls made the salad and wrapped the potatoes to put on the grill and, of course, Donnie teased them the whole time. Warren and Ted, Angie's husband looked after the grilling. I sat on a patio chair and kept an eye on my grandchildren playing in the back yard.

Amy had two girls, Alexa and Annie and Angie had a boy and a girl, Barbara and James.

They were all about the same age and were loud and noisy when they got together.

Alexa, Amy's oldest daughter came and sat beside me. "I miss grandpa," she said.

Tears sprung to my eyes. "I do too honey."

"My mom said he is in heaven, watching over us. Is that true grandma?"

"Yes," I replied. I waited to see where this conversation was going.

"Oh good," she said and left to chase her sister.

I looked up to the heavens. *Jim you would have loved this day.* In spite of everything I knew Jim loved his children and grandchildren and they were important to him.

After we finished eating and cleaning up, Angie and Amy took their tired little ones home. Donnie and I sat at the table talking. "I got the phone number of that Larry guy from Brian and called him yesterday, He told me to take whatever we wanted. Mom, he started to cry. I am going up to the cabin to get the boat and motor tomorrow. Is there anything you want from there?"

"Take whatever you feel is valuable or important. Some of those items belonged to your grandparents. He can have the cabin Donnie, but I'm sure as hell not letting him keep everything in it."

"Do you hate dad for what he did?"

"Hate is a strong word. I don't hate him; I just don't like him very much right now."

It took several more days of hard work to sort and dispose of the things in the house. *That's what you get for not moving in twenty five years. Some of this stuff should have been thrown out years ago.*

Jim had thousands of dollars invested in tools. Donnie and my son-in-law's kept what they wanted, the rest Donnie sold privately to some of the mechanics he worked with. Naturally that money went to Brian for the estate. In the end Angie took the dining room suite.

I kept the couch, two end tables, television set, our bedroom suite, the kitchen table and chairs, and most of the dishes and pots and pan. The pictures and more decorative items went into storage. The girls and I talked about having a garage sale later in the summer.

I wasn't prepared for the house to sell as fast as it did. Three or four couples looked and one immediately made an offer. Brian looked after completion of the sale. Thankfully, I got the asking price which went a long ways to paying off Jim's debts.

After the Auction sale I took the money to Brian. Donnie sold the boat and motor to a friend of his and I gave Brian that too.

He went through the cheques then handed me back the one made out for the boat. "You will need something to live on until your pension cheques start coming from the government. This will be our little secret."

"Is this legal?"

"Actually it is. This cheque is made out in Donnie's name and I have already had him endorse the back of it. Neither the boat nor the motor were mentioned in Jim's will so I assume it was yours not his."

Thank you was all I could say. I was down to my last ten dollars and too proud to borrow from my kids. I know any one of them would have given me what I needed but I couldn't bring myself to ask.

CHAPTER TWELVE

One day, out of curiosity and before the house sold I wanted to see what Jim had done with our money. In the back of my mind, I thought maybe Larry McAdams would offer me some help. Before I found the courage to dial I stared at the phone for a long time. I also wanted to talk to him one more time before I had to move. I still had questions that needed to be answered.

"Is this Larry Mc Adams?" I asked the man who answered the phone.

"Yes, that's me," he replied cheerfully.

"This is Lucy Barnes. I was wondering if I could come over and talk to you."

"Of course, Mrs. Barnes, You are always welcome here. I was hoping we could get together. When would you like to do this?" Now his voice was several degrees cooler, but not unfriendly.

"Now?"

"Give me an hour, and then come over. I am in the middle of something, but I should be finished by then."

"I don't know where you live."

"Oh I'm sorry. It's 22 Martin Drive."

"I will see you later then," and hung up. My hand was shaking *Lucy, I really don't know if you should be doing this. I hope you are not opening yourself up to a new world of hurt.*

I arrived early and drove around the block several times before I found the courage to park the car in front of the house and walk up to the front door. The first thing I noticed was the house was located in an upscale neighborhood, the very opposite of the box like houses in the crescent where we lived.

I also noticed this was the house Jim always wanted. It was made of red brick with a white wrap around porch, a two car garage and a circular driveway. Several large weeping willows grew on each side of the entrance to the driveway and someone had planted colorful flowers around the bases of the trees. *Jim must have done that. At one time he liked to work in the dirt. That was another thing he lost interest in over the past few years.*

I felt like getting back into my car and driving away. I couldn't help but wonder if I was better off not knowing what I might find out. Larry McAdams must have seen me drive up because, as soon as I rang the doorbell, the door opened.

"Come in, Mrs. Barnes," he said.

I was speechless. The house, or what I could see of it, was beautiful, certainly far better than what Jim and I had. Our furniture was well worn, and both the interior and exterior needed painting. I had been asking Jim for the last six months to get the paint and I would do it.

"This is gorgeous," I gushed.

"We were comfortable," he replied.

I'll bet you were and at my expense too I muttered to myself.

"Did you do the paintings hanging on the walls? They are beautiful."

"Yes, these are the ones Jim liked. I am an artist and sell my work out of the Rogue Gallery downtown. Come; let's go in to the kitchen. Can I get you something to drink – tea, coffee, water?

"No thank you, I am good," I replied.

I walked into what was my dream kitchen – new stainless steel appliances, marble counter tops and more cupboard space than one person could possibly use.

Mr. McAdams had coffee made and, rather than appear rude, I accepted a cup. We sat across from each other at a small table nestled in the breakfast nook.

"What can I do for you today Mrs. Barnes?"

I struggled to get the words out. "Tell me where and how you and Jim met? I am having a hard time reconciling you two as a couple."

"Please call me Larry. I met James at an investment seminar a friend of mine was putting on. When it was over, a group of us, including James went to a nearby coffee shop. One by one the others left until there was only the two of us remaining. We hit it off and talked for another hour or so. James talked about you and his children, but I sensed he was conflicted about something.

We met several more times after that. James knew from the beginning I was gay and had have been out of the closet since I was a teenager. On our fourth date, if I may call them that, I invited James back to my apartment and seduced him. By now I knew James was gay, but had yet to admit it to himself.

That night he cried and told me that his world finally felt right. He knew all of his life he felt different than most men but married young, fathered three children but was still confused. Later he told me that the nights with me made him the happiest he had ever been in his life.

His words were hitting me like a sledge hammer but I tried not to let him see how they were affecting me.

"If you knew he was a married man and father why did you pursue him? Didn't you think how this revelation would affect his family?

He shrugged his shoulders. "No, they didn't concern me."

"How long were you together," I asked.

"Five years."

That was about the time Jim lost interest in me. He

continued to be the perfect father but had shut me out of his life.

"You told me the two of you were married?"

"Yes, it was more of a formality than official. He was already married to you, but we had a ceremony in front of witnesses. You do realize Lucy that bigamy is not allowed in this country?"

"I do realize that Larry," I snapped at him. "But I want to know if the ceremony is legally binding." I had no idea what the laws were concerning two men.

"I don't know if it would stand up in a court of law, but we made the commitment, 'until death do us part' to each other."

I sat there staring at my coffee cup. "I don't understand. I don't know what to think and I don't know how to deal with this."

"I can understand that," he said, placing his hand over mine. "James loved you and your children with all his heart, but what we felt for each other was different. I wanted him to tell you how he felt about me and why, but he didn't want to hurt you."

"How considerate of him," I replied sarcastically.

"Lucy, the fact that James was gay was not a choice he made. He was born that way and when he met me, I gave him permission to act upon and recognize his feelings. What is the old saying? "You can't help who you fall in love with."

"Don't try and placate me Mr. McAdams. Do you have any idea what this has done to me and my children? To support your "lifestyle" Jim put us deeply in debt. I have to sell the house to cover those debts and, after twenty-five years, I end up homeless and broke. He chose you over me."

Larry was quiet. "I am sorry Lucy. I had no idea of your financial situation. James never let on that he had financial problems. I would ask him what was bothering him and he would tell me not to worry, he had everything under control.

"Well he didn't, did he? I have lost everything." At one point I thought of asking him for help but now there was no way in hell.

"Sorry to hear that but I'm not responsible."

"Doesn't it bother you that you took what belonged to me and our children?"

"I don't see it that way. This was an investment in our future. Property is always a good investment. Why did you come here today? What did you hope to accomplish?"

"I don't know. I guess I needed to see for myself and try to understand that side of Jim I didn't know."

"And...."

"This," motioning around me "was not what I expected."

"Anything else?"

"I wanted to see what our inheritance bought."

"Surely you don't blame me? James and I bought and renovated this house together. He said this was his dream home."

"Pardon me for asking, but how much did you contribute to this investment you are talking about?"

He didn't answer me.

"Just as I thought, he came up with the financing, and you helped him spend it. This house was your idea, not his. Jim preferred things plain and simple not something as this pretentious. Other than the outside I am sure very little of this was his idea." I pushed my chair back and stood up. "I have to go."

"Lucy, I think you need to know James was with me the evening before he died. I think he had finally made up his mind to tell you about us."

I sat down again. "How was he when he left?" Did he give you any inkling that something was wrong?"

"No, only that he had a headache and that he had been having them every day for the past week."

"Jim has suffered from migraines for years. What I don't understand is why didn't he say something or tell me they were getting worse?"

"He didn't say a word to me either. If I had known something was seriously wrong, I would have made him go to a doctor.

Before you leave Mrs. Barnes, there is one more thing we need to talk about. Why did your son go up to the cabin, remove most of the furniture and take the boat, motor and trailer? I am not pleased with that and my lawyer will be talking to yours."

"Didn't he call you first?"

"Yes, but I didn't think he would take me literally."

"Why shouldn't he?" I challenged him. "What he took belonged to my family. What is it you are trying to tell me? Jim left you the cabin that's all."

"What do you mean, just the cabin? I'm not interested in that old shack. I am going to tear it down and develop the property. It is prime recreational land and will be easy to sell. James thought it was a good idea too, and we were going to do it together."

"What you don't understand Mr. McAdams," I said pointing my finger at him, "is that Jim didn't own the property. That land is in an irrevocable trust for my family. My grandfather made sure that the lake would stay the way it is. He owned all of the one side."

"But you have a cabin on it?"

"Yes we do. We pay one dollar a year rent and the taxes. I am sure you will be asked to move the cabin off, but that is something you will have to take up with the trust's lawyers."

"I will fight you on this," he sputtered, his face turning red.

"Go ahead, but it won't do you any good."

"What am I supposed to do now? I have people wanting to build a resort. I have already accepted advances from them."

"I don't know, that's not my problem," I replied, "You will have to figure that out for yourself. I suggest you return the money and admit you made a mistake about the land being for sale."

Then I asked, "Did you ever love Jim? Or did you prey upon a lonely conflicted man who was willing to do whatever you asked? Did he talk about the lake property, and you saw him as a way to make a fast buck? He was willing to give up a hell of a lot for you."

Once again, he never answered me.

"Just as I thought, I pity you Mr. McAdams. You are going to end up a lonely old man and no matter how hard you try, you will never have what Jim and I shared. We built a life together and raised a family. You can keep your big house and fancy car. Jim and I didn't need all of this to be happy."

I started walking to the door. "Lucy," he called out. "We aren't finished yet. I can't let you leave when you are so upset."

"I am fine," I replied. "From now on, I don't want to hear from or see you. It is best that you leave me and my children alone. I could care less whether you are gay or straight. You are a despicable man and, if you want any more information, you can talk to my lawyer."

I let myself out the door, got into my car and drove home. *I wonder what I would have said if Jim had told me about Larry. Maybe it was better left unsaid.*

* * *

When I got home I felt physically and mentally exhausted. I locked my door, climbed into bed and stayed there for the next two days. I ignored my phone, and when the kids came to the door, I told them I was okay and wanted to be left alone.

During that time, I did a lot of thinking. Sex had never been a high priority in Jim's life, more so after Donnie was born. *Is this what Larry offered him? Did he ever love me? Did I somehow fail to measure up to his expectations?*

I called Cee Cee and asked her to come over. "I need to talk to you."

"No problem honey, I will be there in a few minutes."

When she arrived I looked at her. "How could Jim do this to me?"

She took my hands in hers. "What did he do to you? Do you think he planned on having an aneurysm and dying when he had everything to live for? Do you think he wished for an existence without you, your children and his grandchildren? Do you honestly think he did this on purpose?

Think about it Lucy. What are you really mad about – the

fact that Jim died or that he was gay?"

I thought about this for several seconds. "It's hard to sort one from the other. I feel like I should have known all of these things and done something about them." I answered.

"Could you have known he had an aneurysm?"

"Of course not, I'm not a doctor. In fact he had a check up for work not that long ago.''

"If you had known Jim had a lover what would you have done?"

"I think I would have been angry, but set him free if that's what he wanted. He stopped making love to me five years ago, and the last time was because I begged him to. When I look back our marriage was over a long time ago, but neither one of us wanted to admit it. We stayed together for the kids' sake."

"So where does that leave you?"

I thought for a long time. "I'm angry about the fact left me a financial mess to clean up and now I have to sell our home to pay his debts."

"What could you have done about that?"

"I could have asked more questions. I didn't even know how much money Jim made. I had no idea what the bills were each month or how much our mortgage was. Maybe If I had paid more attention, I would have seen what was happening.

I was content. He gave me as much money as I needed every month and more if I asked for it. Jim liked to be in control, and didn't like being questioned. I should have begun to realize that we were in debt."

"How can you blame yourself for that?"

"I can't Cee Cee. If I had questioned him he would have told me, "you look after the house and the children I will look after the rest" like he always did. After a while I decided knowing our financial situation wasn't worth the argument we had every time I asked. You know how stubborn he could be."

Tears fell from my eyes. "I miss him so much – his laugh, his being home at night and the fact I could reach out and touch him if I woke up afraid, and know I was safe. I was happy in my own little world and not once did I think it would change."

"I know honey. So are you saying his being gay isn't really that important? What makes you the angriest is the debt he left behind?"

"I guess I am. What I don't know is how to move on from here? I don't know where to start. I've never worked outside of the home like so many women do."

"Lucy you are a strong capable woman. It will take time, but you will emerge from this darkness into the light again."

"If you say so…."

"Give it time and be patient. My old daddy used to say

"when a door closes another opens."

I started to laugh. "You know your daddy never said such a thing. Do you have anything else you can quote?"

She giggled. "He always used to tell me 'you got this girl.'"

"You made that up."

"I am trying to say that whatever happens from now on you can handle. Life has thrown you a curve, but you will be okay."

I threw my arms around her. "I love you Cee Cee. What would I do without you?"

After she left, I sat there for a long time. *She is right. I can handle whatever comes along today and worry about tomorrow when it gets here. Jim didn't do this on purpose. He didn't plan on dying and leaving me with all of his debts. I think I could have handled knowing he was gay, but not that he was committed to Larry McAdams. She is right. I have handled what life has thrown at me these past few months, and I know I can handle what comes next.*

I miss you Jim and I will never stop loving you. Please understand that my life isn't over and I must see what the future holds.

As I sat there, a feeling of peace came over me. It was if Jim was saying "You got this girl. Be happy."

CHAPTER THIRTEEN

The sale of the house was finalized the next week and Amy found me a cute little one bed room apartment in an old converted mansion.

When I handed the house keys to the new owners I told them, "This is just a house. What will make it a home are the memories you build inside these walls. Some will be happy, and some will be sad. Cherish every one of them."

It hurt to drive away that day from the only home I knew. Memories of my life as a young mother to a grandmother filled the rooms.

I was still angry at Jim "I hope you are satisfied now," I screamed at him. "Too bad you weren't man enough to be honest with me and your children."

After Brian completed Jim's estate there was ten thousand dollars left. I divided the money into four equal parts. At first my kids refused to take the money, but I insisted. Although it was a small amount I made sure they received an inheritance from their dad. I had to let them know that Larry McAdams hadn't taken everything away from them. Jim's pension amounted to four- hundred dollars a month and helped pay the rent on my new apartment.

One thing I noticed and didn't like was the change in the attitude of my kids, especially Donnie. They went from asking what I thought, to telling me what to do. For the first time I realized how much Donnie took after his dad. When they couldn't get their own way they resorted to bullying.

At first it was subtle – what did you do today mom, to why did you do that? I put it down to the stress we had been under. Donnie was the worst. More than once I told him, "It's not what you say, but how you say it that upsets me."

Once I moved, he began stopping by at odd times of the day. "Just checking to see if you need anything mom." After a while, I began to feel smothered, He was doing the same thing Jim did to me all of our married life. I felt as though he was questioning my every word and every action and holding me accountable if he didn't agree.

Now when I think back over this time, I realize the mistake I made, and, if I had a chance to do it over, I would have handled the situation differently.

The whole experience was like a bad dream. Unconsciously, I had stepped back and handed them complete control. Somehow I gave them the impression I wasn't capable of making any decisions for myself – that I needed their approval.

Moving into my apartment wasn't as traumatic as I thought it would be. After the turmoil of the last few months I was excited about having a place to call my own. There was a lot less room than I was used to and so much less to keep clean.

Cee Cee and the kids helped me the day I moved in. The bedroom was too small for my full bedroom suite so I kept the bed, dresser with the mirror, one bedside table and lamp. While I was supervising the placement of the furniture, Cee Cee organized the kitchen, the bathroom and made my bed. I had a growing list of things I needed to buy. I sold a few things I should have kept and kept a few things I didn't need.

There was a tall bay window with a window seat overlooking the side yard. Set into one corner of the same wall was a gas fire place made of white rock. The space above was the perfect spot to put my television set.

The kitchen was small so I put my kitchen table and four chairs between the living room and kitchen to form a dining area. I also kept my comfortable old couch and coffee table. I had hard time deciding if I had too much furniture or if the room appeared cluttered because of all the boxes in the middle of the floor.

After the children left and we were alone Cee Cee asked, "This is a cozy little place. Do you think you will like living here?" Even with the renovations the owners managed to keep the character of the old house intact.

"It's okay," I replied, "but will take some getting used to. I'm glad I brought my older furniture, because that helps me feel more like this is my home."

"I will be right back" she said and disappeared out the door. In a few minutes she was back with a bottle of wine, two long stem glasses and a bouquet of roses. I didn't have a vase so we put the flowers into an empty plastic juice container.

She filled two glasses and we toasted each other. "To new beginnings," she said. "I have an idea. How about we leave what is left to be unpacked and go out for a celebration supper."

"Sounds good to me. Now all I need to do is find a job so I can afford pay the rent on this place." I said.

"Spoil sport; forget about that for tonight okay?"

"Anything you say boss," and I saluted her.

We went to a small Italian restaurant not far from my apartment. The owner seemed to know Cee Cee and insisted we have the special of the day, Veal Parmigiana and Tiramisu for dessert.

After supper and dessert and while we were drinking our coffee she asked, "How are you really doing Lucy? There have been a lot of changes in your life and I know you find change hard."

"You know something Cee Cee; I am going to be fine. Now that I'm not worrying about selling the house and Brian has Jim's estate settled I feel like a weight has been lifted off my shoulders. Did I tell you I went to see Larry McAdams?"

"How did that go?"

"I'm not sure. In spite of all he said I'm not sure if he loved Jim or saw him as a way of advancing his own interests.

In one way I think he used Jim or James as he called him, but in another I think he was as lonely as Jim was. It must be difficult to know you are not like other people, that you will never have a family to call your own."

"Is it possible that Jim was aware of what Larry was doing or was he caught up in the forbidden aspect of their relationship?" she asked.

"That's something I will never know," I replied, "but I do know one thing. He was not happy to find out that he didn't own the property the cabin sat on."

"I thought Jim left that to him."

"Just the cabin, not the land it sat on. My grandfather bought the land on that side of the lake for a dollar an acre and it is held in trust for our family. The cabins you see there all have long term leases with the trust fund. He knew what a treasure the lake was and wanted to keep it that way and he was adamant about not letting it be developed. He wanted everybody to enjoy the area not just the wealthy few."

"Wow, Lucy, I see why that McAdams guy wasn't happy. Was he planning on developing that side of the lake?"

"Yes, and already accepted some money from some land developer. I think he has a mess on his hands now." I grinned at her. "But that doesn't bother me at all. At least my children still have their great-grandfather's legacy."

That night when I went to bed I slept all the way through

and didn't dream about Jim.

I was busy the next couple of days. I made several trips to the storage locker bringing some things to the apartment, taking others back. I got my phone hooked up and managed to keep my old number. I got the cable hooked up for my television and visited my grandchildren every day.

The evenings were long and I allowed myself to be distracted by the T.V. On the cooler evenings I turned the fire place on, wrapped up in a blanket and read.

I kept telling myself *you got this* over and over again.

Then I crashed. One afternoon I walked into my silent, empty apartment and started to cry. I missed my home, my neighborhood, my kids, but most of all I missed Jim. I longed to feel his arms around me, to pick his dirty clothes up from in front of the hamper and to reach over and touch him in the night for reassurance.

The hurt and anger were gone but I missed what we had and mourned for what was lost. Nothing seemed important any more - his sexuality, his partner, or his debts. Jim had been my husband and best friend for over twenty-five years. I loved him and I wanted him back.

After I stopped crying I went into the bedroom, took my photo albums from the closet shelf and carried them back to the living room. I let my mind wander back to our beginning.

CHAPTER FOURTEEN

Jim and I became boyfriend and girlfriend when I was sixteen. We were part of the same group of friends, all of whom were paired up, and we were the odd ones out. I guess you could say we were friends who drifted into a relationship. He was seventeen, nearly eighteen, and I was proud of the fact I was dating "an older man."

Everybody we knew said they were doing IT, but Jim and I agreed we would wait. We fooled around lots of times, but always managed to stop before we got too carried away. .

Then, quite unintentionally, IT happened. We were at a drive-in-movie and for some reason decided we could see better from the back seat. One thing led to another and before we knew it we were making love. When we were finished we organized our clothes, climbed into the front seat and Jim put his arm around me. We were both embarrassed and personally, I was a little disappointed. I could see Jim was very uncomfortable.

"That shouldn't have happened," he said staring straight ahead.

"I know, but what if I get pregnant?" I whispered to him.

"Then I guess I will have to marry you."

We left before the movie was over and I had Jim take me straight home. I didn't know what to think and I was afraid my parents would find out. My dad didn't like Jim. He used to tell me, "There is something off about that boy."

I did my best to ignore his comments. My dad would have found fault with any boy who came near me, especially one as poor as Jim. He wanted me to marry up, to someone who could give me more than he could.

Then one morning, mom walked into the bathroom and caught me throwing up into the toilet. "Are you pregnant?" she bluntly asked me.

"No, I just don't feel good this morning" I tried to tell her, but by the look on her face I knew I wasn't fooling her.

Mom had a mouth like a sailor and she let fly with every expletive she knew, and then some. I didn't hear what she was saying as waves and waves of nausea passed over me.

When I saw Jim at school later that morning, I began to cry.

"What's the matter," he asked.

"I need to talk to you," I replied.

"Can it wait until school is out? Mr. Jones told me if I was late for class one more time, he was going to kick me out. If that happens I won't be able to graduate and will be stuck here for another semester. Meet me at my car, okay?"

Jim was waiting for me when I got to the car. "What did you want to talk about? What's wrong, having trouble with your dad again?"

"I'm pregnant," I blurted out, "and mom knows. I don't know what to do."

"Are you sure?"

"Yes, I have been getting sick every morning for the past two weeks."

He got a funny look on his face. "I guess that answers my question doesn't it?"

We stood there for a long time. Jim stared off into the distance, and I leaned back against the car, my arms wrapped around my middle.

"What do you want to do?" he asked.

"What choice do I have? I am going to have the baby." What I wanted to say was *I want to graduate with my class. I want to move away from here, but I am going to have to quit school and find a job to support me and the baby.* Jim was a senior and only had two months before graduation. I was in grade eleven and hoped to go to University when I was finished high school.

"I said I would marry you if this happened and I'm a man of my word Lucy."

We agreed not to tell anyone. Then once school was over, we would get married. Suddenly I wanted to be alone. "Instead of going to Ella's party tonight I want to go home. I don't feel very well. Can you drop me off?"

"If that's what you want," he replied. His voice was flat, and his face devoid of any emotion. "Get in."

When he stopped in front of my house I got out of the car and ran to the front door. I was glad my parents weren't home because I didn't want them to see what I mess I was. He was eighteen, I was sixteen and we were going to become parents.

Later I heard Jim went to the party, and got so drunk that he passed out on Ella's neighbor's lawn. I can't say I blamed him because that is exactly what I felt like doing.

After that, we couldn't keep our hands off each other. We reasoned that the damage was done so what difference did it make? I realize now we should have taken time to think and talk, but we didn't. Neither one of us were aware of how much our life was about to change.

Several days later mom told dad what she suspected and he was furious. The next time Jim came over, dad screamed at him- something about being hauled up on statutory rape charges. He grabbed Jim and threw him up against the wall, calling him one vile name after another.

I stepped between them, "leave him alone right now. Jim and I have already decided to get married and there isn't much you can say about it."

Dad backed off. "Over my dead body," he sputtered. "Because you are only sixteen years old I do have a say. You need our permission to go ahead with this. What do either one of you know about marriage and raising children? There is more to it than making them."

Mom looked at me, "maybe you and Jim should leave, and I will handle your dad." As we were leaving, my dad swore at Jim again. Mom told him to shut up.

Jim graduated as planned and we got married the first weekend in July. Our wedding wasn't fancy. I wore a white sundress and Jim wore a white shirt and a new pair of jeans. His parents and mine met us at the Town Office, and we were married by a Justice of the Peace. Afterwards dad took us all for supper.

We went to a motel in Gainsford, about twenty miles away, for our wedding night. The next day we moved in with Jim's parents. Years later I found out that dad gave Jim one hundred dollars in case he didn't have enough to pay for the motel room. I will say one thing though sex was a lot more fun after we were married. We made the most of every chance we had.

Jim's dad helped him get a job as an apprentice mechanic at one of the local trucking firms. Right from the beginning of our marriage Jim controlled our money. We paid rent while we lived with his parents. We didn't really go anywhere, nor do anything special. Our friends dropped us because we had nothing in common any more.

Jim usually came home late from work and I got bigger and bigger. When the Doctor told us we were having twins, Jim's dad helped us buy an older home and the two of them renovated it.

We moved in a week before the twins were born- two girls, we named Amy and Angeline. After they were born we argued a lot. I resented being stuck at home with two babies who seemed to cry all the time. When he came home from work Jim was usually tired and wanted to sit and relax. I wanted him to help with girls and give me a break.

One time he yelled at me, "I bring in the money, and your responsibility is to look after the home and the kids." Another time he looked at me and declared, "Why don't you stop complaining about how hard you have it. I didn't ask you to get pregnant."

I retorted sarcastically, "I believe you had something to do with that. This wasn't exactly how I wanted to spend my teenage years either."

"Then you should have kept your legs closed."

"And maybe you should have kept your penis in your pants," I retorted. "You get to leave every day and I am stuck here. If one isn't crying, the other one is."

"I don't know what you expect from me Lucy. Maybe it's time for you to grow up."

That was the first time I realized Jim had a cruel streak in him. After that I tried not to say anything that would upset him. Jim was never physically abusive, but he had a way of cutting me down and making me feel inadequate.

When the girls were eighteen months old I got pregnant with Donnie. That time is still a blur. Jim went away to school for six weeks, and I stayed home with the kids. My morning sickness was worse than it was with the twins. Money was always tight but Jim never complained when I asked him for a little more.

As the kids got older, Jim got better with them. Donnie was his pride and joy. He was always there for their activities, hockey or special events. Sometimes I resented the fact that I did all of the work, and Jim received all the glory.

After Donnie was born our sex life gradually diminished. We went from making love once a week to once a month, and during the last few years of our marriage to having no sex at all.

Jim got his mechanics papers and was promoted to shop foreman. I continued to stay home with the kids, and concentrated on being the best wife and mother I could be.

It took a while, but after the twins were born, my dad finally got over being upset and accepted Jim as his son-in-law. There was a world of hurt between them, but I give Jim credit, he tried to make the most of a bad situation.

Both sets of parents passed away over the years. Jim was close to his dad, and grieved for a long time. We both grieved in separate ways. Jim buried himself in his job and I became more deeply involved with the children's activities. I see now we would have been better off if we had shared our feelings.

As I got older there were times I used to wonder if there was more to life than what we were experiencing. I often wondered if there something we were missing.

I mentioned this to Jim once and he got a funny look on his face. "Why would you be thinking like that? You have me, the kids, and a decent house to live in. I would say you are pretty lucky. What more could you possibly want?"

Another time I suggested getting a part-time job. "A part-time job would give me something to do during the day, while the kids are at school." I told him.

He looked at me with a scowl on his face. "No wife of mine works," he stated. That was the end of that conversation.

I missed the sexual part of our relationship. More than once I tried to talk to him about what I perceived was a problem. "Maybe you should get a checkup," I suggested.

"There is nothing wrong with me." he retorted, "Maybe if you looked after yourself better I would feel more tempted."

I started exercising, and went on a diet but it didn't seem to make any difference. One night I decided to seduce him. I knew the kids were having a camp out at a friend's place so I went shopping and bought a new frilly, black, night gown.

When I crawled into bed I snuggled up to him and ran my hands up and down his body. After several minutes he slapped my hand away. "I'm tired Lucy," he said and then rolled over and turned his back to me. I don't remember ever feeling so hurt or rejected in my life. After he fell asleep I got out of bed and put on my flannel pajamas. I didn't sleep much that night. The next day I threw my new night gown in the garbage.

Jim was always interested in the stock market and investing. When our community college offered a one night workshop on investing I encouraged him to go. After attending that work shop he joined an investment group which met once a week. By the time he came home I was usually in bed and asleep. When I asked questions, his answers were vague or he changed the subject. I was happy he was doing something he enjoyed.

He was still good to me and the kids, but there were times when he seemed completely unapproachable. He distanced himself from me. We stopped talking to each other unless I asked a direct question or we discussed something about the kids. I felt like we were two people living separate lives, but living in the same house. Both of us did our best to put on a good front for the children. I knew our marriage was in trouble but thought eventually we would work out whatever this was- like we had all the other times when we had problems.

I wish I knew then what I know now. I had no idea Jim was struggling with his sexuality. Once I found out, that explained many of the stranger parts of our relationship.

CHAPTER FIFTEEN

Although I was born and raised in this small city I wasn't familiar with the area where my apartment was located. After getting settled I needed to get out and see what there was. I knew there was a park at the end of the street, but what I needed to find was easy access to a grocery store within walking distance. I kept my car, which needed repairs. It was a gas guzzler so I used it only when I needed to.

Across from the park was a strip mall with four shops. One was a grocery store, but as I walked closer, I saw a Help Wanted sign in the window of O'Shea's Coffee House and Bakery. I searched the job listings in the newspaper every day, but either I wasn't qualified or didn't have enough experience.

Maybe I can get a job here. After, all how hard can it be? Maybe I could help with the baking. I'm not afraid to work in the kitchen and wash dishes. Heaven knows I have done enough of that in my life. Being a stay at home mom doesn't leave me with many useable skills. If I don't find something soon I am going to have to give up my apartment and moved in with one of the kids.

The Coffee House was a surprise. It was bright and airy, and smelled of fresh bread and baking and coffee. Pictures of Scotland and of young girls twirling in their kilts hung on the walls. There were two glass counters filled with fresh baking. Between the counters was a space to place orders, and a row of coffee carafes along the back wall. A tray of plaid paper napkins, stir sticks and plastic forks and knives sat on the counter.

There were five round tables with four chairs each in the center of the room, and along the back wall a bench with two tables in front of it. All of the chairs and the bench were covered in the colors of various Scottish tartans.

As I entered the shop, I noticed an older, gray, haired woman busy behind the counter. "Excuse me," I said. "I noticed your sign in the window, what kind of help are you looking for?"

The woman looked up at me with kindest eyes I have ever seen. "I bin lookin' fer someone to look after the front counter, serve the customers and keep the tables clean and tidy."

"Oh. I thought maybe you needed help with the baking." I felt disappointed.

"Are ye looking for a job then?" she asked, with a Scottish lilt to her voice.

"Yes, but I have no experience. To tell you the truth, I have never had a job. I don't think I would be very good working with the public." I turned to leave, but she called me back.

"N'er had a job?"

"No. I was a stay at home mom until my husband passed away several months ago. I ended up having to sell my house and now live in a small apartment on the other side of the park, the one that looks like an old mansion."

"What's yer name dearie?" she asked.

"Lucille Barnes, My friends call me Lucy."

"Bin hard has it?"

I shook my head yes, tears flooding me eyes. *Don't do this Lucy. All you need to do now is blow any chances you might have of getting this job.* I turned my head away so she wouldn't see them.

"'I'm sorry. Sometimes it is still too hard to talk about."

"Bin sick a long time was he?"

"No," I sniffed, "He had a brain aneurysm. It was totally unexpected."

"Oh ye poor dear, any family?"

"Twin girls, Amy and Angie and a son Donnie. They are all grown now and I have four grandchildren, three girls and a boy."

She looked at me again. "Ye must 'ave married young cusn ye don't look old enough to be a grandmother."

"I was sixteen, he was eighteen." *I don't know why I am telling her all of this.*

She looked at me for several seconds as if trying to make a decision. "The job is yours if'n you want it. I was thinking of a school girl, but at least ye will be dependable. It's not as if ye can't learn what to do. Ye need to know I kin only pay ye minimum wage few now."

"I'll take it. When do you want me to start?" This felt almost too good to be true.

"Come after one o'clock tomorrow. The lunch rush slows down about then and I kin show ye what ye have to do. By the way me name is Clara Donovan."

"The name on the outside says O'Shea. Are you the owner?"

"Aye, that was me maiden name. Donovan's sounded more like a bar than a coffee house."

I stuck out me hand. "I am pleased to meet you Clara. I'll see you tomorrow then. Oh I forgot what should I wear?'

"A pair of black pants and a white blouse if'n ye have that. If not, something presentable."

For the first time in a long time I felt hopeful. *Maybe my luck was finally going to change*

CHAPTER SIXTEEN

It was a good thing Clara had tons of patience because she needed every ounce of it with me. I was so out of my comfort zone. First I needed to learn what she sold, and the prices. Not only were there were various types of coffee – lattes, cappuccinos, decaf, espresso, organic and Columbian, there was non-fat milk, soya milk, two percent, half and half cream, and skim milk plus all of the different flavorings to mix with the coffee. To me coffee was coffee.

Finally she taped notes to the back counter with the instructions for preparing each coffee printed on them. That was a life saver. Each day she offered a soup and sandwich special and it was almost impossible to mess up those orders. That made my job much easier and I already knew the names of the pastries she offered. The hardest part of my job was counting back change on an order until she showed me an easier way.

I hated the fact she made me wear a sign which read "have patience, I'm in training" for the first two weeks I was there. Now I believe that sign made people easier to deal with when I got their order wrong.

In the beginning I was overwhelmed and made a lot of mistakes, but not once did she get cross with me. For the first week my feet and back ached so much I felt like quitting, but I didn't

It wasn't long before I noticed a pattern to her sales. The same people stopped for their morning coffee on their way to work. At noon those who worked nearby came for lunch, and then mid-morning and mid-afternoon the same group of older people came every day. Clara knew most of them well and frequently inquired about their health and well-being. They trusted her and in return, I saw how much she genuinely cared for them. I loved my job and the atmosphere, and gradually overcame my lack of confidence and low self-esteem. The pay wasn't great but, if I was careful, I had enough to live on.

During those first weeks, there was only one customer who upset me. "I asked for a Columbian with two regular creams and one sugar."

We were busy. "I am sorry," I said, "I will replace it for you."

"If you can't get it right the first time, how do I know you will the next? Anybody should be able to figure it out; after all you don't have to be a rocket scientist to work here. Where's Clara, she'll fix it for me properly?"

I took the cup from his hand, dumped it out into the sink and fixed him a new one. Handing the cup to him I said, "It's on the house but maybe you should taste it before you leave the counter." *What a jerk. I wonder, who does he think he is?*

He took a small sip. "It will do, "he grumbled.

I don't know why he upset me so much. Maybe it was something in his tone of voice but whatever it was, I felt intimidated. In one way he reminded me of Jim and how he often made me feel small and stupid. *If I can't even get this man's order for a simple cup of coffee right, how am I going to get the rest of my life right?*

Just then Clara came out of the back, "Who peed in yer corn flakes this morning Jason? If'n yer are going to speak to me staff like that, then don't bother coming back. Just' cause ye got up on the wrong side of the bed this mornin, ye don't need to take it out on others. Go sit down and drink yer coffee like a good boy."

He glared at Clara, but did as he was told.

Then she turned to me. "Don't let him get to you. Underneath that rough exterior there be the heart of a pussy cat. Every once in a while I has to put him in 'is place. He takes life too seriously."

"What's with him anyway?" I grumbled.

"Not my story to tell. If'n ye want to know, ye'll have to ask him yerself. If'n somebody tells me somethin' in confidence that's where it stays. I don't believe in gossip."

We were taking a break one afternoon after the lunch rush, because, for a short period of time, the store was empty of customers. "Lucy, ye need to stop brooding o'er the death of your husband. Me church has a bereavement group that meets twice a month. I kin take you if'n you have mind to go. I bin going since me daughter died of the cancer two years ago. I found it helped a lot."

"That obvious is it?" I asked.

"Nay, just to me. It's like there be a dark cloud hanging o'er yer head."

"Thanks for asking Clara, but no thanks. I don't want to tell my sad story to anybody, least of all a group of strangers."

"Well, if'n you change yer mind, let me know."

"I won't, all I need is time."

She looked at me, "Aye that helps, but sharin' helps too."

One thing I learned about Clara, if she wanted you to do something, she had a subtle way of convincing you that it was your idea in the first place. She left me alone for a while then casually mentioned. "I be takin cookies fer the group tonight if'n you want to come."

"No, Clara, but thanks for asking."

"Ye could gain a lot by going. If ye don't go, ye will never know...."

Every two weeks as faithful as a clock, she mentioned going to the group meeting. Finally I had enough. "Okay I will go with you this one time just to keep you happy."

She grinned, "Ye won't be sorry."

We'll see about that I muttered under my breath, *Maybe*

she will leave me alone after this. I will go this one time to keep her happy then tell her I wasn't comfortable.

"Good." She added, "I'll pick ye up around six thirty."

"Okay," I agreed.

The gathering was held in the meeting room of the local Anglican church, and wouldn't you know it, the first person I saw when we walked in was that Jason guy. Immediately my defenses went up.

When he saw us, he walked over, gave Clara a kiss on the cheek and said to me, "Welcome to our group. While we are waiting for the others to arrive, help yourself to a coffee and one of Clara's excellent cookies."

I couldn't resist. "Is it Columbian with two regular creams and one sugar?" I asked.

He looked at me and then it dawned on him. His face turned red. "I guess I had that coming," he replied sheepishly, "I apologize for being rude to you the last time we met."

"I accept your apology," I teased him.

Just then Clara came rushing over with two Styrofoam cups of coffee in her hand. "We'll sit by the door if'n ye decide to leave early."

"First maybe I should introduce you two. Jason, this here be Lucy who ye met at the coffee shop. Lucy this here be Jason," then she added, "Her husband passed away suddenly a few months ago."

He smiled at me and said "well then, you have come to the right place."

While we were waiting for the others to arrive, I took a good look at him. He was tall, slim, and very attractive looking, with long dark hair pulled back into a short pony tail. He had light tan skin, but what struck me the most were his sad dark brown eyes. The last time I saw him he was wearing a charcoal gray suit, but tonight he wore black jeans with a black shirt, with a heavy gold cross hanging around his neck. His voice was deep, calm and soothing, but there was something about him that made me feel unsettled.

Jason turned out to be a gentle, compassionate group leader. People spoke freely. Instead of saying, "you should do this or you should do that," he asked, "what do you think you should do, or what do you want to do?"

After the meeting ended he walked over and held out his hand. "How about we start over? My name is Jason Knight."

"Lucille Barnes" I replied, shaking his hand. "My friends call me Lucy."

"Friends?" he asked.

I laughed, "Yes friends until you holler at me again."

Turning to Clara he asked "would the two of you like to go for coffee and we can get to know each other better?'

"No, not me," I replied. I turned to Clara, "If you don't mind, I would just as soon go home."

"No problem," Jason replied, and then turning to Clara he asked "Am I forgiven? I was having a bad day."

"Aye this time, but don't let it happen again." They both laughed. Clearly there was some sort of understanding between them.

By the time I got to Clara's car tears were streaming down my face. She gave me a hug. "A good cry cleanses yer soul. Get in I'll take ye home."

On the way I commented, "He talked about forgiveness for our own sake so we can move forward and accept this as part of our life story, but I don't know if I am ready for that yet."

"Aye maybe not now, but one day ye will be."

It was as though the universe and Clara conspired against me, because, after that night, my life began to change again.

"

CHAPTER SEVENTEEN

After attending that first meeting a small voice inside my head kept telling me I needed this. So two weeks later, when Clara mentioned we should go again, I agreed her.

"Feelin' better about this are ye?" she asked as she handed me a box filled with oatmeal, raisin, chocolate chip cookies to carry inside.

"I admit it helps to know that I'm not the only one going through a hard time, and that everyone there feels exactly the same way I do."

"Aye, there is that," she replied,

I learned a lot each time I went. There are stages of grief – denial, anger, bargaining, depression and finally acceptance. I skipped the bargaining stage, unlike many of the others who had pleaded or tried to make a deal with God, only to lose their loved one in the end. I began to understand I was caught up in the anger/depression cycle.

My life irrevocably changed the day Jim died. I accepted the fact that he was gay, but what I was having trouble dealing with was that he provided for Larry McAdams and I was forced to give up everything that was important to me - my home, my life, and the trust of my children. They would always think I kept secrets from them. Once I became a widow, our closest friends stopped including me in their activities, and others, when they heard Jim was gay, dropped me all together. I often wondered if for some reason they felt threatened by his sexuality.

I sat. I listened, but held back the impulse to share my story. When I look back on that time I realize I was afraid of what the others would think of me. Other than telling Cee Cee I hadn't expressed my deepest feeling to anyone. It was bad enough I saw myself as a failure as a woman and as a wife I didn't need others in the group seeing me that way. Now I realize how twisted my thinking was.

About six weeks later, at the end of the meeting, Jason approached me. "Can I apologize again, and buy you a cup of coffee?"

That night I didn't want to go back to my lonely empty apartment and cry, like I usually did. The one bright spot in my life was the meetings. Over time, they were helping me realize there was more to life than grieving for a loved one and how life used to be.

"Yes," I replied, surprising us both.

"Did I hear you right? The ice queen said yes?"

"You did, but why are you calling me the ice queen?"

He looked embarrassed, "I don't really know it just slipped off my tongue. You have a wall around you that suggests you are unapproachable and that your life stopped one day and froze in time. There is a little coffee shop around the corner called Dockers, How about I meet you there in about twenty minutes. I have to lock up here first."

I didn't like hearing what he called me and almost changed my mind, but the invitation meant I could stay away from my apartment for a while longer. I parked in front of the café and waited in my car until I saw him ride up and park a black Harley Davidson. He wore a black, studded, leather jacket and gathered his collar length hair into a small pony tail. In fact, he reminded me of one of those bikers you see in the movies. I got out of my car and stood beside it until he saw me.

"You ride a motorcycle?"

"Yes, why? What difference does it make?"

"I don't know. I usually don't pay attention to what people drive. You surprised me that's all. I pictured you as a sedan driving kind of guy not a biker."

He laughed and winked at me. "When you get to know me better, you will find I am full of surprises."

And what makes you think I am going to get to know you better, I thought. *This is a one-time thing.*

He held the café door open for me, then put his hand on the small of my back and ushered me to one of the booths along the back wall.

Inside the café looked like one of those diners you see in a 50's movie. There was a long counter with red vinyl stools and a window which led to the kitchen. Red vinyl booths lined the windows and the back.

One man sat on a stool chatting with the waitress. In one

of the booths a couple sat across from each other holding hands and drinking coffee. The black and white tiled floor was well worn where people walked.

"Have you had supper?"

"No I closed late tonight and had to rush to get to the meeting on time. I know you don't like to be interrupted by people who are late."

The waitress ambled over with two menus. "What can I get you to drink," she asked.

We both replied "coffee please."

I was surprised to see the menu was a mix of western and Chinese food selections. An older Chinese man hurried out of the kitchen and rushed to our table. Jason stood up and shook hands with him. It was easy to see they were good friends.

"Mr. Jason, Where have you been, I haven't seen you for a very long time and never with such a pretty lady?"

I felt my face turn red. "This is my friend Lucy Barnes," Jason replied. "Lucy this is my friend Ben Chang. His son and I went to college together."

I stood and shook his hand. "Pleased to meet you," I said.

"What can I get for you tonight?" Ben asked.

"Allow me," Jason said. "Bring us two bowls of your delicious Wor Won Ton soup?"

"My pleasure," Ben nodded and hurried back to the kitchen.

"What is Wor Won Ton soup? I have never tasted it before."

"Then you are in for a treat. Ben makes the best in town and I should know I have tried every one of them. I hope you aren't allergic to shrimp?" he added as an afterthought.

"No, I am fine," I replied.

Minutes later the waitress appeared with two steaming bowls of soup filled with vegetables, noodles and shrimp with green onions floating on the top.

"Go ahead, try it. If you don't like it I will you order something else."

The soup was delicious and filling. I found Jason easy to talk to. While we ate, we talked about small things. I told him about my children and grandchildren. Finally I found enough courage to ask, "what made you decide to start running this group?"

He got a funny look on his face. "My fiancée and I lived together for nearly six years. We had a little girl we named Chloe, and the two of them were the love of my life. One day I came home and they were gone, as well as most of the furniture in the house.

We were going through a rough patch, but I still don't understand why she left. We fought bitterly over Chloe. I was going to take her to court for full custody of Chloe and then the accident happened."

"I am so sorry Jason," I said, putting my hand on top of his, but he didn't notice his mind was far away.

"When she heard what I was planning, she ran away. It was raining heavily and she was on an unfamiliar road, missed the approach to a bridge and landed in the river. They both drowned. She was leaving with our daughter and trying to get as far away from me as she could. For a long time I blamed myself."

I didn't know what to say. "How long ago did this happen?"

"About six years ago. After that, I bought my motorcycle and travelled a lot. I had some pretty rough years and did a few things I wasn't proud of, but finally got my head on straight. I figured with my experiences I could help others learn to deal with their grief. I went to a couple of weekend retreats, took some credit courses at night at the community college, and then started our group. I thought that, if I had some place to go and talk about my grief, accepting their death would have been easier, but then I wouldn't have the good and bad experiences either."

"It's hard either way. To get on to a happier subject what do you do for a living?"

"I'm an Investment Broker with a group here in town."

My heart seemed to stop. I glanced at my watch, and realized it was after ten. I stood up. "Thank you for the coffee and the soup". The walls were closing in on me and I needed some air. *Why did he have to have a job that involves investments? Did he know Jim and Larry McAdams?*

"Don't tell me I have scared you off with my serious talk?"

"No, it's getting late and I have to open early in the morning," I lied.

I put ten dollars on the table and practically ran from the coffee shop to my car and drove home as fast as I could. Only when I was back in my apartment, did I feel like I could breathe again.

I tossed and turned all night, but sometime in the small hours of the morning I realized my pain would never go away, but I could learn to live with it. Each time I closed my eyes I recalled the sadness and loneliness in Jason's eyes. *Is that what people see when the look at me? Is that why he calls me the ice queen?*

.

CHAPTER EIGHTEEN

The next morning, when I walked into work, Clara looked at me and asked "why have ye' been crying? What 'appened last night? Did Jason say something that hurt yer feelings?"

"I don't want to talk about it," I brusquely replied.

"There be no call to bite me head off young lady," She snapped back. "but if'n you decide to talk I'll be in the kitchen."

"I'm sorry Clara. I didn't mean to be short with you."

Just then the bell over the door tinkled and the first of our early morning customers walked in effectively putting an end to our conversation.

Ten minutes later, Jason came in for his usual Columbian with two cream and one sugar. I didn't look at him as I handed him his cup.

"What happened last night?" he asked. "Everything was great and then suddenly you took off like a scared rabbit. Did I say or do anything that upset you? If I did, I apologize."

"No, it wasn't that, "I lied. "When I get overtired, I am

prone to headaches and I could feel one starting."

He studied me for several seconds. "I don't believe you, but will accept your explanation for now." Then he had to move aside, so I could serve the line of customers growing behind him. Instead of leaving as he usually did, he went and sat at one of the small round tables until the lineup of customers was done.

"Clara," he called out. "I am going to borrow Lucy for five minutes if that's okay with you?"

"Do ye want to talk ta him?" she asked me. "I kin ask him to leave if'n you want me to."

"It's okay." I poured myself a cup of black coffee and sat down across from him.

"Talk to me Lucy. Tell me what happened last night? You come to the meetings, but you sit and listen, and never say a word. I called you the ice queen because your expression never changes. You never smile. The rare times you do, you light up the room."

I sat there staring into my cup.

"Tell me why Lucy," he asked gently.

"You said you were an Investment Broker?"

"Yes," he answered warily. "What's that got to do with you leaving so abruptly?"

"Do you know Larry McAdams?"

"Not really. Just to see him, but I heard he came into some money and property recently when his partner passed away. I met his partner once, seemed like a decent guy. Why?"

"I can't do this Jason," I pushed my chair back and stood up to leave.

He put out his hand to stop me. "Whatever happened is keeping you in a dark place. It's not healthy for you mentally or emotionally. Talk to me."

My small voice was screaming at me. *Tell him Lucy then he won't want anything to do with you*

I sat down again and took a deep breath. "That decent guy you met with Larry McAdams was my husband Jim. We were married twenty-five years. That money and property Larry came into rightfully belonged to me and my children."

He stared at me for a minute and then a look of comprehension flitted across his face. He reached for my hand and took it in his. "I am so sorry."

"Don't be." I replied, pulling my hand away. "It's all in the past. What's done is done."

At that moment the door opened and two of our regular customers came in. "Two coffees' and two of them chocolate covered doughnuts Lucy." They spotted Jason and grinned, "Whenever you have time that is, we don't want to interrupt you."

"I have to get back to work," I said. As I stood up, I saw a look of pity on Jason's face. "I don't need you feeling sorry for me either," I added as I walked away.

Jason left a few minutes later. "Will I see you at the next meeting?" he asked before leaving

"I don't know," I replied.

When we were closing, Clara asked me, "what was that all about Lucy, the talk 'tween you and Jason?"

I told her. "Jason and I went for coffee after the meeting last night .Everything was going good until he told me he was an Investment Broker. Suddenly I pictured him being as sleazy as Larry Mc Adams. Then I was afraid he knew Jim. I started having a panic attack and had to get out of there."

"Okay, I kin understand that," she said

"He told me about his girlfriend and his daughter. His eyes were so sad. I felt as though he was still broken inside. Is that how people see me Clara, - sad, broken and in need of their pity?"

"Maybe if'n they knew yer story they would. To me yer are like a broken china plate, finding the pieces and putting yerself back together, one piece at a time. Right now yer trying to figure out where the pieces are and how they fit. At this point yer not sure what the picture will look like when ye get done. Ye've had a hard time Lucy, but life goes on. Ye still have many happy years ahead of ye yet."

I walked over and hugged her. "I have been called a lot of

things Clara, but never a broken plate."

She put her hands on each side of my face. "Yer a beautiful person inside and out and soon I hope to see who ye are when yer all back together." She took her hands down. "Go home. It's been a long day."

Jadon didn't come around for the next couple of days, but when he did I looked him in the eye and apologized, "I am sorry for acting like an idiot, I think I overreacted."

He smiled at me, "so are we good then?"

I giggled. "Yes, we are good." *Why are you giggling like a school girl? This is ridiculous and no way for a lady of your age to act.*

"Hey lady, when do I get my coffee?" an angry voice behind Jason called out. "I'm in a hurry and haven't got all day."

Jason picked up his coffee, smiled at me, then turned and left the shop.

I put on my brightest smile, "and what can I get you sir?" I asked.

Suddenly I felt hope, like a tiny bit of light had penetrated the gloom I lived with.

CHAPTER NINETEEN

Jason and I became friends and fell into the routine of meeting for coffee after the meetings. Letting my guard down around him wasn't easy. He challenged me to enjoy life, being with him was fun, and I began to feel like my life had purpose again. I was cautious about introducing him to my children, because I didn't know how Donnie would react. I was sure the girls would like him but lately Donnie seemed to disapprove of everything I said or did.

Jason often told me stories about the places he had been and the people he met. Some were funny, others were sad. At group, he was kind, patient and considerate. He knew how to relate to each person and how to validate their feelings. People opened up to him and expressed themselves in ways they normally wouldn't have.

I began to talk and share part of my story with the others, but never once talked about Jim's sexuality. In private, Jason encouraged me to talk about this with the group but I couldn't. I felt this was too private to speak openly about. I didn't want to explain to strangers that I was too naïve to know what was happening.

"Lucy," he often told me "this is an important part of your grieving process. You have nothing to be ashamed or embarrassed about."

"What good will it do except dredge up more feelings of inadequacy and the question how could you not know or why didn't Jim tell you," I answered back. "The only answers would be "no I didn't suspect" and "I don't know." *Even if I had any idea Jim was gay I wouldn't have known what to look for.*

Nor did we discuss Jason's role as an Investment Broker. That was his private business. It was hard enough knowing he met and liked Jim as a close friend of Larry McAdams.

He taught me how to laugh, to find joy in the smallest of things, and to stop being so serious.   As the days passed, I felt myself becoming attracted to him.

Even Clara noticed I was happier. "He be good for ye Lucy. I kin see he has feelings for ye too."

"I like him as a friend Clara, but I'm not ready to have another man in my life and probably never will be."

"Ye can't go through the rest of yer life not trusting men. Not every man is like yer Jim."

"I know, but I don't want to take that chance again. Once was enough to feel that kind of hurt and betrayal."

"I didn't say ye had to love him, but you kin have sex with 'im. Men are kind of nice to have around for that."

My mouth fell open. "What did you say?"

"Ye heard me. If'n you don't take a chance, ye will never know if ye need a man around or not."

I didn't have an answer for her so I quickly changed the topic. One thing about Clara, when she had something to say, she didn't hold back. I knew she was right, but wasn't about to admit anything to her.

Jason and I cared for each other but I wasn't ready to commit to anyone. Surviving on my terms meant exploring and experiencing what was out there for me. The only person who seemed to understand where I was coming from was Cee Cee.

Another thing that bothered me was the fact I was three years older than Jason. In my generation liking a younger man was taboo. There was even a name for that type of woman – cougar I think she was called. It made more sense to look an older man who could, and would, take care of me.

* * *

I never knew from one day to the next what Jason would think of doing. One evening we stopped at the playground in the park across the street, and he pushed me on the swings like I was a little kid. He challenged me to ride on the merry-go-round then pushed it so fast he fell down. I don't know when I have laughed so hard. If anybody was watching they would have thought we were crazy.

Another time, as we drove past a bowling alley, I mentioned I had never been bowling. Two days later I am in a pair of rented green shoes, and he is explaining that the objective of the game was to knock down the pins at the other end of the alley.

"How hard can that be?" I said to him. I walked up to the line, spread my feet apart and rolled the ball from between them. I wasn't prepared for how heavy the ball was and it wobbled about three feet and rolled into the gutter.

"I'm going to try that again" I told him. I did and got the same result. I heard him snickering behind my back but when I turned around, he had a straight face.

"Do you want me to show you how it's done?" he asked.

"Don't you dare laugh at me," I said, picking up my third ball and rolling it harder. This time it nearly reached the pins before it fell off.

My turn," he said and knocked all the pins down at one time. "Strike," he called out."

"Show off."

We played three games and by the time we finished, I managed to knock down a pin or two each time.

"Told you it wasn't hard," I gloated. Being the gentleman he was, he agreed with me.

One other Sunday morning he showed up at my apartment while I was still in bed. "What on earth are you doing here so early this morning? You know this is the only day I can sleep in."

"You have ten minutes to get ready. We're going on a picnic."

"I am not," I declared. "You can't waltz in here and tell

me what to do. I have things I need to do today."

"They will wait. It's a glorious day and too nice to stay in this stuffy apartment. If you aren't ready, I'll leave without you."

"I suppose you expect me to ride on your motorcycle too?"

"No, I brought my car today. Hurry up, we are burning daylight." *Now he is quoting John Wayne, I wonder what he is up to.*

When we got outside, I was surprised. He was driving an older, red, mustang convertible with black leather seats and the top was down.

How did he know this was a fantasy of mine – riding in a convertible with the top down, the wind blowing through my hair.

He opened the passenger door for me and I noticed a large wicker picnic basket in the back seat. He buckled me in. then walked around the back of the car and got in the driver's seat.

"Do you want me to put the top up?"

"No leave it down. By the way where are we going?"

"You tell me. I want to see this lake you are always telling me about."

"I don't think that's a good idea Jason."

"Of course, it is. It's just a piece of property Lucy, and I want to see why it's important to you. Maybe this will bring back some good memories of the times you spent there."

"I wonder if Larry McAdams has moved the cabin off yet." Under the terms of Jim's will, that's all he was allowed to do."

"There is only one way to find out for sure," he said, putting the car in gear.

We drove west out of town for about an hour then turned onto the gravel road which led to the Rochester Lake. Jason stopped at the top of a small hill and looked out over the area. The lake was calm, without a ripple on it.

"This is beautiful. I can see why developers want to latch on to this place. It's a little piece of heaven stuck in the middle of nowhere." Jason stated.

"Isn't it? That's the very reason my grandfather decided to stop developers from coming in and ruining it. He wanted to keep this area the way it is. Drive downs the hill, take a left turn, then follow the road around the bend, and we will come to where our cabin was."

When I saw the cabin was still standing I breathed a sigh of relief. The place looked forlorn and deserted and the grass needed cutting. Clearly Larry McAdams wasn't taking care of it. The boat dock was exactly the way we left it the last time we were here. It must have been in the water all winter because it leaned to one side.

"Can we go inside?' Jason asked. "This place is

awesome."

"I don't see why not, obviously there hasn't been anybody here for a long time."

The main cabin was two stories tall and made of hand hewn logs with several additions over the years. The door was unlocked and when we went inside it smelled musty and dusty. All of the rooms were empty except for the propane stove and fridge in the kitchen, and the large wood box beside the stone fireplace.

Don't get all maudlin now Lucy. This cabin is just an empty building. All that remain are the memories you have.

"You know what," Jason said. "There is nothing that says we can't force Larry to move this cabin off and we could build a new one. I bet he will say we can have it back, that he has no use for the building without the land. Maybe he will sell it back to us. Let me talk to him and see what he has to say."

"Go ahead if you think it will do any good. By the way what's this we stuff" I teased him.

He got a funny look on his face. "Sorry, I meant you and your children. How are you doing Lucy, this must be hard on you?"

"Surprisingly well, all things considered. *Returning here isn't as hard as I thought it would be. Besides even if Larry would sell it back, I wouldn't be able to afford it. I don't have that kind of money.* Are you ready to eat yet? Somebody dragged me out of my apartment early without breakfast and I am hungry. Follow me; I know where there is a great spot for a picnic."

Jason went back to the car to get the picnic basket and I wandered down toward the lake. There was a spot down the beach, not too far from the cabin where the trees came to the edge of the sandy beach and an old fallen tree lay along the edge.

"I used to come here to think. I would sit on that tree and watch the sun setting on the water. It was quiet and peaceful, but I was still close enough to hear the kids if they called me."

Jason stood there admiring the view. "I don't know about you but suddenly I'm starving."

"Is that all you ever think of is your stomach?"

"No, not all the time Lucy," he winked at me, "sometimes I have other thoughts too."

I felt my face turn red. "Why Jason Knight, are you flirting with me?"

Now his face turned red. He took the blanket he brought from the car and spread it out on the one small patch of grass by the trees. The menu for the day was fried chicken, several different salads and a bottle of wine. For our wine he brought clear plastic glasses.

I laughed, "is this really the best you could do, chicken from Barneys Chicken Palace?'

"I don't cook," he replied.

While we ate, I did most of the talking. I regaled him with stories about the neighbors and the antics and messes the kids got into.

"I am going to miss coming out here." I told him. "I have been coming here since I was a kid. Then I brought my children and never once thought that I wouldn't be able to the same for my grandchildren."

"Maybe one day you will be able to come back."

"I am not sure if I really want to. It won't be the same."

"Yes you do Lucy. This is still a place your family will always be part of. Don't let Larry McAdams take away all that was good in your life."

"You are right. I never thought of it that way. This place is still my grandfather's legacy for my kids and grandchildren. Now that I don't have the house to return to, this will be the place although it would be a shame to see the cabin go to waste."

Jason abruptly stood up, grabbed my hand and pulled me to my feet. "Why don't we tidy up here, then you can show me around? I noticed a sign back there that read Marksman Trail. Is that something special?"

I folded the blanket while Jason packed what was left of the food and our garbage into the picnic basket.

"Yes" I explained to him, "there are all kinds of trails through the bushes, each named after the pioneer who first settled that piece of land. If we had driven further and turned at the next road, we would have come to a day picnic site and a boat launch. Some say there are fish in this lake, but I have yet to catch one."

Jason took my hand and we walked further down the beach. Memories flooded my mind and Jason was very quiet. *He is right; there are too many good memories here to lose. If the cabin is moved, we can always find a way to build another one.*

When we returned to our spot Jason reached for the picnic basket and I picked up the blanket. Then I heard him say softly, "turn around Lucy."

I turned to look at him. He put a hand on each side of my face and kissed me. At that moment I realized I had been waiting for this. I dropped the blanket, put my arms around him and pulled him toward me.

When the kiss ended he stepped back. "I better get you home before I get carried away, and start something I won't want to stop." He took my hand and we walked back to the car.

"I wasn't prepared for that," I said to him.

"Neither was I. I have been thinking about doing that for a long time and the setting was perfect. I couldn't help myself."

"You need to understand one thing. I am not ready to get involved with anybody. I honestly don't know if I will ever be again."

"It was just a kiss Lucy, and a very nice one at that. This place is magical and I couldn't see any harm in kissing the beautiful woman by my side."

CHAPTER TWENTY

The more time I spent with Jason, the more confused I became. When Jim and I were married we were young and in lust. Over time I came to love him. Later in our marriage I sometimes thought of him as my best friend with benefits.

This was entirely different. My feelings for Jason ran deeper than that and, within a short period of time, he became an important part of my life. He accepted me for me and didn't try to change who I was. Instead he encouraged me to figure out who I wanted to be. He made me laugh, and he let me cry.

Jason never pushed. I knew he wanted to make love to me and I wanted him too, but I was afraid. If I wasn't "good enough" for Jim, I couldn't bear the thought of being rejected by Jason too. *What if he is disappointed in me? There must be something wrong with me if Jim had to turn to somebody else, especially a man. I don't understand what happened or what I did wrong.*

I don't know how many times I wondered what it would be like to make love to Jason, but didn't have the courage to follow through.

One rainy evening we were watching a movie and carrying on like teenagers in the back seat of a car when the familiar pangs of panic began to crawl through me. His arms felt too confining and I couldn't breathe. I put both hands on his chest and pushed him away.

He got a puzzled look on his face. "What's going on Lucy?"

I could barely breathe. "I can't do this" I gasped and scurried to the other end of the couch. I drew my knees up to my chest and wrapped my arms around them desperately willing the panicky feelings to go away.

"Lucy, I'm not going to force you to do something you aren't ready for. The time and place is in your hands, but I will tell you waiting is getting harder and harder. I want you."

I smiled at him. "I know" I answered softly, "Why me Jason? Why choose me when you can have any woman you want. I am three years older than you, as dowdy as they come and an emotional mess, or do you look for people that need fixing?"

"Stop right now. You are beautiful to me. You are like a caterpillar emerging from its cocoon and turning into a beautiful butterfly. I am a normal heterosexual man who happens to be attracted to you."

"Oh so now I'm a caterpillar," I giggled. "You certainly have a way with words. You must have been talking to Clara, because a few days ago she compared me to a broken plate."

"Someday Lucy you will see the truth. You have done your duty as a wife and a mother, now you have been given a second chance to experience all you have missed in your life."

I didn't know what to say. I never thought of my life in those terms.

"The thing is Lucy," he continued, "You need to learn to trust others. Your love and marriage with Jim was the first part of your life now you get to decide what you want to do with the next part. All of those flaws you talk about mean nothing to me. You are a beautiful, intelligent woman and I want to be with you."

I didn't know what to say, He got up, tuned off the television and the lamp on the end table leaving only the flames of the fireplace for light. "Come over here and let me hold you."

He sat down again and held out his arms to me. I moved from my end of the couch and put my head on his shoulder. I stared into the flickering flames once again feeling safe.

"It so happens I happen to like older women and you remind me of my mother." he said.

"What? Now you are comparing me to your mother?"

He laughed. "Yes, you are soft, warm, and cuddly in all the right places."

For a moment I felt insulted but then realized he was teasing me. "You are intelligent, funny and have that special quality that endears you to people," he continued. "I love how excited you get when you try something new, it's like you are seeing everything for the first time. You brought back the sunshine into my life which I thought was gone forever. Tell me you're about marriage to Jim."

"There isn't much to tell."

"Tell me anyway."

"The first time Jim and I had sex I got pregnant. I was sixteen and he was almost eighteen. Jim did the right thing and we got married. The twins were born six months later. Now I see we were too young, and had too many babies too quickly.

We were your typical young couple. There was never enough money and, once the kids came along, we didn't make enough time for each other. Jim took every overtime shift he could so we could make ends meet."

"Did you ever work outside of your home?"

"No, I wasn't allowed to."

"That's a strange choice of words, "allowed to.""

"Jim had the idea that he had to be in control everything. He saw himself as head of the house and what he said went. Now I wonder if that was a way of proving his masculinity.

He would tell me "I'll look after the money, you look after the children." His dad was very much the same way. I was the mom who baked cookies for the bake sale, helped in the class room, went on field trips and joined the PTA.

When the kids got older, they brought their friends to our house There always seemed to be one or two extras around.

Jim always made time for Donnie, the girls not so much, but he made a point of attending their dance recitals or school functions.

You have to understand Jason, I was happy. At first I rebelled, but finally accepted the fact that this was my role. My life was my husband, children and my home. I worked hard at doing my best for them."

"When did things begin to change?"

"When Jim joined that Investment group. After the first few years our sex life became less and less. I remember asking him about it once. His response was he was usually too tired by the time he got home from work. I thought that was a normal part of being married."

"Oh, the old I am too tired routine. Usually it's the other way around."

I hit him on the arm. "The truth was many times I agreed with Jim. I wanted more children but he made sure that didn't happen. He had a vasectomy after Donnie was born and somehow forgot to tell me."

"How did you feel about that?"

"I was hurt and angry. I don't think he would have ever told me except for the fact I kept trying to have another baby but couldn't get pregnant. That's when he told me that he got himself fixed."

"How did that make you feel?"

"Stop trying to analyze me. I was devastated but did what

I always did, accepted the fact and moved on. I didn't have much of a choice."

Jason got up and went into the kitchen. He returned with a half empty bottle of wine and two glasses. "We might as well finish this."

"Will you be able to drive home if we drink this?"

"I could always stay here," he grinned.

He must have seen the look on my face. "Just kidding, Yes, I will be okay. Where were we? You mentioned that Jim began to change after he joined that investment group. How?"

"Little things like buying new dress clothes, staying out late, and phone calls he would walk out of the room to take. One at a time these things didn't seem like much, but I think he was probably beginning to get more involved with Larry McAdams. I even tried to seduce him but stopped when he told me, after twenty-five years of marriage sex with me wasn't that important anymore."

"Did you suspect anything?"

"Once or twice I wondered if he had a girlfriend tucked away some place."

"You didn't ask?"

"No. I didn't want to know. Funny thing I was right. He was seeing somebody else, only it was a man." I began to cry.

Jason put down his wine glass and wrapped his arms tighter around me. "You can't blame yourself Lucy; you had no way of knowing Jim was gay."

"I know that now. I tried so hard to please him, but I never stood a chance once Larry came into the picture. If he hadn't died, I may have never found out."

We sat like that for a long time. I must have fallen asleep, because the next thing I knew Jason was covering me with a blanket.

"I want to stay and make love to you, but this isn't the right time. I'm going home before I forget my good intentions and get carried away."

I wanted him to stay but couldn't find the words. "Perhaps you are right. Thank you for being so patient with me. Jim was the only man I ever slept with, and he rejected me. I can't bear the thought of you doing that too. I wasn't enough for him, and I don't know if I will ever be good enough for anybody else."

Jason didn't say anything. He kissed me on the forehead. "I'll see you tomorrow."

I sat looking at the fire for a long time. My fear of being hurt again was overwhelming, but Jason was slowly and surely whittling away at my defenses. I was becoming comfortable with him touching me. I wanted to take our relationship further, but backed away each time the opportunity presented itself. Tonight was a good example.

I got off the couch and climbed into my bed clothes and

all. *I never knew you were such a coward Lucille Barnes. Next time say yes, and see what happens.*

CHAPTER TWENTY ONE

Don't get me wrong. Although I was developing some deep feelings for Jason I didn't want our relationship to get too serious. He was always surprising me, like the afternoon he called me just before I left work.

"I want to take you out for supper tonight. Put on your jeans and a warm jacket. I will be there by six thirty."

"Where are we going?"

"It's a surprise."

That it was. When we left my apartment I expected to see his car but instead his motorcycle was parked beside the curb. "You chariot awaits my lady."

"Are you serious? No way am I getting on that thing."

"Why not? You will be perfectly safe."

"I am too old for this, besides I have never been on a motorcycle in my life. I don't have a clue what to do. What if I fall off?"

"You won't. Besides I happen to be a very good driver. Here, put this on first," he said handing me a helmet, then he helped me climb on and then sat in front of me.

"Put your arms around me and hang on – tighter" he said at my feeble attempt. "Now lean when I do."

I hung on to him for dear life. I have never been so scared, yet felt so exhilarated at the same time. We rode to a small restaurant about five miles out of the city and set well back from the main road. I must have been down this road a hundred times on my way to the lake and not seen the small sign on the side of the road.

When he stopped and I got my shaky legs back on the ground, I was giggling like a school girl

He looked at me. "What's so funny?"

"First of all, that I survived and secondly, that was awesome. I have never been so scared yet this made me feel like a kid again."

He looked at me and whispered, "You should laugh more often." He reached up, took my helmet off and hung it on the handle bar of the bike.

Jason was right. I suddenly realized that somewhere in my life I forgot how to laugh. Jason was teaching me to enjoy myself again.

"Is this part of your Grief Therapy program?" I teased him.

"No. I like you Lucy. This is part of the Jason therapy to win your heart."

I wasn't sure how to take that comment. To change the subject I asked "I didn't know this place existed. What is it?"

"The Barbecue Shack. I come here to eat quite often. Ted serves the best barbecued ribs in the country."

The Barbecue shack was a non-descript, red cedar building nestled in the trees. Colorful picnic tables were scattered around the lawn, many of them occupied with young families. The delicious aroma of barbecued meat filled the air.

I was surprised when we went inside. Three long trestle tables with benches on either side ran the length of the building. Just inside the door was a counter with a take-out menu printed on the back wall. Two young girls were working behind the counter and ahead of us, were several people waiting for their orders.

When it was our turn Jason stepped up to the counter and ordered two baby back rib meals with the works. "What do you want to drink," he asked.

"Iced tea will be fine."

"And two iced tea" he told the server at the counter. He pulled forty dollars out of his pocket and handed it to her. "Keep the change, you girls deserve it." In return, she handed him a plastic sign with the number twenty four on it.

"Now we wait," he said.

Within five minutes our number was called. Jason picked up the tray and we went back outside to one of the picnic tables. The tray also held napkins, packs of ketchup, packages of plastic dinnerware, and several wipes for our hands. Inside each Styrofoam container was a large slab of barbecued ribs, coleslaw and fries

Neither of us said much while we ate. When we finished, Jason dutifully put the boxes and plastic tableware into a garbage can, the plastic glasses into a recycling bin, and the tray on top of a low counter outside the door.

"Well, what do you think? Was that worth the scary motorcycle ride?"

"Yes it was," I declared, "it wasn't the motorcycle that scared me, it was who was driving, but he did okay too. Why haven't I heard about this place? The food is delicious?"

He winked at me, "I guess that means we will have to come again."

When we got back to my apartment I was laughing. This time I knew I was safe on his bike, and I let myself enjoy the ride. He helped me off, and when he helped me take of my helmet he kissed me.

"It's early yet. Would you like to come up for coffee?" I asked

"Now that is one invitation I can't refuse, but I can't stay long. I am expecting a phone call later this evening. Remember I also have a business to attend to."

We went upstairs and I put the coffee on.

"You are something else Lucy Barnes." He came up behind me and kissed the side of my neck. I wasn't sure what to say.

"Jason," I started to tell him that I wasn't ready to have a man in my life again when there was a loud pounding on the door.

"Open up this door mom."

When I opened it, Donnie pushed past me. I knew by looking at him he was angry. He walked over, and stood in front of Jason.

"Who are you and what are you doing here?" he demanded.

Then he turned to me, "Who is this guy and what is he doing here in your apartment?"

Before I could get a word out Jason extended his hand. "I am Jason Knight, a friend of your mom's. You must be Lucy's son Donnie. She has told me a lot about you and your sisters."

Donnie ignored his outstretched hand and stared at me, waiting for an answer.

"Jason and I went out for supper this evening. What are you doing here anyway?"

"You weren't answering your phone and I got worried. I came over to see if you were okay and when I got here, I saw you getting off a motorcycle and this guy climbing all over you."

"He wasn't climbing all over me. What you saw was a simple little kiss, and none of your business."

. I looked at Jason, "I think you better go and let me handle this. Thank you for supper and the ride. I enjoyed myself."

As soon as the door closed behind Jason, I looked at Donnie. I was furious. "How dare you come in here and act like a spoiled brat."

"Who is he mom? You two seemed awfully friendly to me."

"He is a friend and the leader of the Grief counselling group I go to. There is nothing going on between us. "

"That's not the impression I got. As far as I am concerned that looked a little too friendly to me. I think he has more on his mind than helping you get over dad. Are you sleeping with him?"

"How dare you talk to me like that?" I felt like slapping him." And if I am, which I'm not, I don't need your permission, and besides, what I do is none of your business." I opened the door and said "get out."

"Take it easy mom. We need to talk about this."

"No we don't Donnie, not now, or not ever, now leave."

He slammed the door on his way out. I locked it, then slid down to the floor and cried. *Is this nightmare ever going to end? First Jim controlled my life and now Donnie thinks he can. When am I going to be able to do what I want?*

My phone rang several times after that but, when I looked and saw it was Donnie, I didn't answer it. After the fifth call,

I saw it was Amy calling.

"Are you okay mom."

"Yes, I am fine. If Donnie put you up to this tell him not to call me again tonight. I have nothing to say to him."

"He is as mad as hell. Do you want me to come over?

"I am fine Amy. I am going to bed. I have to work tomorrow. We'll talk about this another time. Good night" and I hung up.

"The last thing I need now is to have trouble with the kids. Why can't they leave me alone" I screamed out to the empty room. "I am so tired of fighting every one and for every little thing. When is it my turn to be happy?

I felt the dark mantle of depression settle over my shoulders and surround me once again.

CHAPTER TWENTY TWO

The next day after work, I had barely closed the door on my apartment when my cell phone rang. My first thought was that something was wrong. The only people who had my number were my children, Cee Cee, Clara and Jason.

"Hello," I answered. I had butterflies in my stomach and was instantly on alert.

"It's me" Jason said, "Are you okay?"

I laughed. "You scared me. I thought something happened. Every time my cell phone rings I think the worst."

"I tried your house, but there was no answer. Then I got worried because you are usually home by five thirty. What are you doing tonight?"

"I don't have any plans. Why?"

"A friend of mine and his band are playing at Sonny's Western Bar and Grill, and I thought you might like to put on your dancing shoes and come with me."

"I will go and listen, but just so you know, I don't dance very well. In fact, I'm not sure if I know how to act in public anymore. I have only been to a bar once in my life, and that was to celebrate my eighteenth birthday."

I don't think Jason realized I was serious. Jim had rarely taken me out, other than to his work Christmas parties and for supper the odd time. Every once in a while I suggested we got to one of the neighborhood functions but he refused. After a while I simply quit suggesting.

Now it was Jason's turn to laugh. "Don't worry about it. By the time the evening is over, most people don't act very well. I'll pick you up around eight."

It was already seven fifteen and I had to hurry to go ready. Usually I came straight home after work, but tonight I stopped at the grocery store first. I didn't feel like cooking, so I treated myself to a hamburger while I was there.

The feelings I was developing for Jason were now beyond the point of friendship. I cared for him, and this frightened me because sometimes I felt as though I was being disloyal to Jim.

I had a fast shower and dressed quickly. I hated to keep anybody waiting. By the time I was finished, there was a knock on my door.

"You are early," I said as I opened it, but it wasn't Jason standing there, it was Donnie.

"Come in. I thought you were somebody else."

"Who, - that same guy who was here the other night?"

"Yes, as a matter of fact."

"What are you doing mom? Dad hasn't been gone a year and you are running around with some guy half your age."

"His name is Jason, and he is not half my age, only three years younger. What's with the third degree and why are you here? Its Friday night, why aren't you out with your buddies as usual?"

I saw that something was troubling him. "Do you want to tell me what's bothering you?"

"I need to know something. Did you ever love dad?"

"Of course I did, Donnie and I still do. He was my life, but he is gone. I have been forced to continue without him. That wasn't my choice, but that's the way it is. Nothing is going to change what happened."

"Did you love him even the last few years, when he was cheating on you with that Larry guy?"

"I didn't know that. I will admit things weren't very good between us, but I thought it was a phase married couples went through. Our marriage vows did say for better or for worse."

"If he had told you he was gay, would you have stayed with him?"

"I honestly don't know. That is one of the questions I will never have an answer to.   Why are you so concerned?"

"I want to know how serious you are about this Jason guy."

There was a knock on the door and before I could answer it, Jason walked in. He stopped, looked at Donnie and me.

"I can come back later," he said. "I didn't know your son was here. I don't want to interrupt anything."

Instantly Donnie's demeanor changed. "Never mind, I was just leaving. I guess that answers my question."

"What question? I don't know what you are talking about." I started to say, but he had already stormed out, slamming the door behind him.

Jason looked at me, "what was that all about?"

"Nothing just Donnie being Donnie. Don't worry about it."

I knew Jason wanted to know more, but I didn't want to talk about it. Donnie and I had to work this out our own way and getting Jason more involved wasn't going to help.

We drove about twenty miles out of town, and then pulled into a nearly full parking lot. I think we got one of the last parking spots available. As soon as I opened the car door, I heard the thump of a base guitar and the hum of voices.

"My friends are saving us a seat," he said, taking my hand and leading me to the door.

The building's exterior resembled a barn with a wide veranda across the front. Inside along one side there was a long bar with wooden stools and a door which probably led to the kitchen. A small stage was set up at the end of the room. There was a juke box and wooden dance floor which took up the rest of the back area. The front part of the room was filled with round wooden tables with four chairs each. Lit wagon wheels hung from the ceiling, and rodeo pictures decorated the walls. The room was crowded and noisy.

He led me through the crowd, past the bar to a large round table close to the stage. When we got there, he introduced me to the three men sitting there. "These are the guys with the band" Pointing from one to the other he introduced them "Trey plays lead guitar, Buffy plays drums and Joe likes to think he can sing,"

. Then he introduced me, "this is my girlfriend Lucy."

Trey moved over to make room for us and Jason and I sat down.

"What would you like to drink Lucy?" he asked.

"A beer will be fine."

Jason called the waitress over, "a Corona for the lady, a draft for me and, and bring another round for the table."

Trey peered around Jason at me and asked "did Jason tell you he tries to play the guitar?"

"No, he hasn't mentioned it. Why?"

"If he does, don't encourage him. He isn't very good."

Trey grinned, "Not only that, he likes to think he can sing too. Sometimes we feel sorry for him and let him play one or two sets with us to soothe his ego."

Jason punched him in the shoulder. "Not fair man. You

sure know how to hit a guy below the belt. You know I can out play you any day." Then he winked at me. "I am a man of many talents" I felt my face turn red.

Trey got an innocent look on his face and I had to laugh.

This was a side of Jason I hadn't seen before. I sat back watched and listened, as he talked with his friends. He was smiling and animated. The juke box was loud and people were laughing and enjoying themselves. I felt myself begin to relax.

Shortly after we arrived, the band left the table and got up on the stage. I was surprised at how good they were. They played songs I recognized from the radio. The small dance floor quickly became crowded. Then the music changed and everybody rushed to the dance floor and formed lines

"Do you know how to line dance?" Jason shouted above the noise.

"I don't even know what that is," I shouted back.

He grabbed my hand and pulled me to my feet. "This is as good a time as any to learn. You can't come to a country and western bar without knowing how to line dance. Follow me."

We went to the back of the line. As I watched, I saw a pattern to the steps and a rhythm to the music. "It's simple actually, do the same thing as the person in front of you." Jason whispered into my ear.

I have two left feet and, at the best of times, getting them coordinated wasn't easy. I wanted to sit down before I made a fool of myself.

The music stopped, and nobody moved. When the music started up again Jason said, "You are doing great, and soon the steps will come. Watch me and do what I do." By the time the band began to play the third song I felt like a pro.

When that dance ended I was laughing. Jason kissed me on the forehead and whispered, "You did great." We went back to our table and the next time people began to line up, I grabbed Jason's hand and pulled him onto the dance floor. *I don't remember the last time I had so much fun.*

Jason knew a lot of people and many stopped by to say hello. I sat back and admired the ease he spoke with them. Some he introduced to me, others he didn't. One or two I recognized from our bereavement group. Tonight they looked happy. When the band began to play a slow song, he suggested we dance.

"I would rather not," I told him. "I don't waltz very well."

He stood up, held out his hand and replied "that is no excuse. I think it is time you learned."

There wasn't much room to move, so we basically stood in one place and swayed back and forth. I put my head on his shoulder and he rested his chin on top of my mine.

The band played a set of three slow romantic songs and we remained in our spot on the dance floor while the other couples moved around us. Being in his arms felt natural and right and I was content to stay there.

I don't know how to describe the feeling, but I felt shift something inside of me. I wasn't afraid anymore and was ready to take our relationship to the next step.

Jason must have sensed the change too because, when the music ended, he led me back to the table and whispered, "I think it is time for us to get out of here."

I looked at the clock over the bar and it was past midnight."

"Yes." I agreed.

Neither one of us spoke much on the drive home. When we got back to my apartment I asked Jason if he wanted to come upstairs.

He looked over at me, "If I do Lucy, I intend to be here all night."

"I know." I took his hand and led him up the stairs.

"Are you sure?" he asked as I unlocked the door.

"No, but I want you to stay anyway."

Once inside he locked the door, backed me up to it and we kissed passionately. When we came up for air, I took his hand and led him to the bedroom. "Come with me." I whispered.

When I saw the bed, I froze. Jason sensed the change in me right away. He walked over, sat on the edge of the bed and patted the spot beside him.

"Come, sit down and tell me what is going on in that pretty head of yours."

I didn't know what to say.

"Why tonight Lucy?" he quietly asked, taking my hand in his.

"When Donnie was here, he wanted to know if I really loved Jim."

"What did you tell him?"

"I told him when Jim was alive he was my life, but he is gone and I have to continue living. Tonight, when we were dancing, I realized that living is being with you. You make me feel alive and bring back feelings I haven't had for a long time."

Jason was quiet.

"I want this and you. I am ready but…."

"But what?"

I started to giggle like I always do when I am nervous. He got a strange look on his face.

"It's been so long I don't know if I remember what to do. What if you are disappointed in me.?"

He let go of my hand and started to laugh. Then he put his hand under my chin, and turned my face toward him and kissed me.

"Somebody once told me it's like riding a bicycle, you never forget."

"Seriously, here I am spilling out my deepest fear and that is all you can say?"

He shrugged his shoulders and the tension in the room disappeared.

"Kiss me again." I said, "And I will see if I can remember."

When a man makes love to a woman she wants to feel special. That night Jason made me feel as though I was a goddess. He was a patient yet demanding lover, never asking for more than I was willing to give. When I was with Jim, he always seemed to be in a hurry and many times I was left feeling used. In Jason's arms I experienced feelings I never felt before and rose to heights I never knew were possible.

Afterwards, I lay with my head on his shoulder; his arms wrapped around me. For no reason, I began to cry. I tried to stop the tears, but failed.

"Why are you crying? Did I hurt you?'

"No. it's just that I have never felt like this before. I don't know how to explain this to you. Up until tonight I felt that part of me was missing; now I feel thoroughly loved and complete." *A sudden thought passed through my mind. Is this how Jim felt when Larry McAdams made love to him?*

I don't know why, but I expected Jason to laugh at me but

instead he gently asked," how long has it been Lucy since somebody made love to you. I don't mean had sex, but really loved you the way you deserved?"

"I don't know. I can't remember .One day Jim would be loving and affectionate, the next he would push me away. I put my feelings in a box and followed his lead. After he rejected my advances several times, I gave up and waited for him to turn to me, but that all stopped about five years before he passed away. Now that I know what I know, that must have been the time he started to see Larry McAdams."

His arms tightened around me. "You are amazing and your Jim was a fool. He didn't know what he was missing," he chuckled.

I lay in his arms like a contented kitten. Soon I felt Jason relax and fall asleep. I nestled into his arms and drifted away too.

Sometime later Jason woke me up and we made love again. This time I was as eager as he was. I drifted back to sleep sated and content. All too soon I heard him whisper "I have to go Lucy, I have an early morning appointment, but can I come back tonight?"

"Yes and every night after that too." For the first time since Jim died I felt truly happy.

The next time Cee Cee came to visit I told her about Jason and I making love. I expected her to censure me but she surprised me by saying, "took you long enough." Then she asked "does he make you happy?"

'Yes. I didn't know I could feel this way about another person. He makes me feel alive and safe. He accepts me for who I am, not as he wants me to be. I tried not to fall in love with him but I did."

"Good, you deserve to be happy. Have you told your kids about Jason yet? What do they think?"

"No, I haven't said anything yet but they know I have gone out with him" I confessed.

"How did that go?"

"How do you think it went? Donnie has already voiced his objections about me seeing Jason. He was here when Jason arrived to take me out one evening. I don't want to fight with them Cee Cee, I know they won't approve."

"Lucy, you do what you want. This is your life. Live it for you and be happy. After all you've been through you deserve a second chance at happiness."

* * *

Being with Jason prompted me to start paying more attention to myself. The first thing I did was make an appointment to get my long hair cut shorter. I had worn the same style since high school. When he saw me the first time he said "Wow."

"Is that a good "wow" or a bad one?" His response unnerved me.

"You look amazing. Come over here and I will show you how much."

I giggled. The last time I cut my hair this short Jim was furious. He ranted and raved for days at how much money I had wasted.

Walking back and forth to work and being on my feet all day whittled away some of the excess weight I carried. Cee Cee took me shopping and with the help of a few good sale racks I bought some new clothes for work and was able to add to my meager wardrobe.

On the drive home she said "I like this new Lucy. I have never seen you so happy."

"I am happy Cee Cee, for the first time in a long time. Jason is an amazing man and he treats me as though I am somebody special not another piece of old furniture taking up space."

As I said that a dark thought flitted through my mind. *You know all good things come to an end. Life is too good to be true. Everything would be perfect if I could share my love for Jason with my children but Donnie has made it perfectly clear that is not going to happen.*

.CHAPTER TWENTY THREE

After that Jason spent every night at my place. For the next while we lived in our own little world. He brought me red roses to celebrate our two week anniversary, another time several of my favorite chocolate bars. When I was sick with the flu, he brought me chicken soup from Clara's. I ate it anyway because I didn't have the heart to tell him I hated the taste. Every night he made love to me, and kissed me awake every morning. More than once, I pushed the thought out of my mind that this was too good to last.

The twins were celebrating their twenty-seventh birthday and the family was gathering at Amy's house. I decided this was as good time as any for them to meet Jason. Besides, I had some good news to share. Larry McAdams wanted nothing to do with the cabin and sold it back to me for a dollar. I didn't ask, but I am sure Jason had a lot to do with that.

"Come with me." I urged him. "I am sure Donnie has had time to think and cooled down by now. I want them to get to know what a wonderful person you are, and how much we care for each other."

"I'm not sure this is such a good idea Lucy. Have you told them about us yet?"

"No, but they are aware that we have been seeing each other. I think this would be a good time as any for all of you to know each other."

He was hesitant, but finally agreed to come with me. I chose to ignore the idea that he was having second thoughts. I wish I had listened to him.

Once we arrived at Amy's front door he held back. "I think you should go in alone. When you are ready, phone and I will come get you."

"No way," I laughed, "you are coming with me. "I grabbed his hand, rang the doorbell and walked in like I always do.

The house was noisy. My grandchildren were chasing each other and squealing at the top of their lungs. Then little Annie spotted me.

"Grandma," she cried out. I picked her up and swung her around. "I didn't see you for a long time." I gave her a hug then she wiggled out of my arms and charged into the living room.

"Grandma's here. She has a man with her. Can we have cake now?"

I took Jason's hand and followed her. There was dead silence when we walked into the living room. I looked from one to the other and saw the hostility in their eyes.

I broke the silence. "I would like you to meet Jason Knight. Since we are all together I thought this was a good time for you to meet him, and for Jason to meet my family."

"Is he the one you are sleeping with?" Donnie asked.

I didn't know what to say. Certainly this wasn't what I expected.

"Mom, we know the two of you are sleeping together. Donnie told us about Jason quite a while ago and he has seen his car parked at your place all night. How can you do this to us?" Angie asked.

"Do what? I don't know what you are talking about."

"Dad isn't even cold in his grave and you are living with another man."

I didn't know what to say. I felt sick to my stomach. I thought they would be happy for us, for me. *What could I say to make them understand?*

Donnie walked over and stood in front of Jason, his hands on his hips. For some unknown reason I noticed they were the same height. "Get out. You are not welcome here."

"Stop being an ass Donnie," I told him, but he acted as though he didn't hear me. "If Jason isn't welcome here, I guess I'm not either," I continued and turned to leave.

"You stay where you are," Donnie yelled at me, "we need to talk to you. He's the only one leaving right now."

I looked over at Jason. "I think I should go Lucy. It will be easier for everybody if I leave. Call me when you are ready to come home." He kissed me on the forehead and walked toward the door.

I watched him leave and when the door closed behind him, I turned toward my kids. "That was completely uncalled for. You didn't have to treat him that way. Jason is a good man."

"Why not?" Donnie retorted. "If he is such a good man, why has he turned my mother into a whore?"

I was hurt and angry. I couldn't believe my son was calling me names. I sat down on the nearest chair and tried to calm myself. "Maybe you had better tell me what this is all about." No way was I going to let them see how much they were hurting me. "If you have something to say, you had better say it before I walk out of here."

They all started talking to me at once. I put my hand up to stop them, "One at a time if you want me to answer your questions."

Amy was the first to speak. "I heard you were going to some kind of group therapy thing. Did you have to spread out family secrets all over town?"

I tried to answer. "Amy, it's not a secret. Your dad was gay, but you shouldn't let that bother you. He was a good man and he loved you with all his heart. Don't be ashamed of him. What you need to remember is that he was a human being like the rest of us. Who he was, is more important than his sexual orientation." Donnie stood across the room his arms crossed, staring at me, his eyes filled with disgust.

Then Angie spoke up. "We never see you because you

are too busy with him. You never come around. Every time I ask you to babysit you have an excuse. It's like you don't love us anymore. Last week I phoned you three times. I had a Doctor's appointment then was going shopping with a friend. I wanted you to stay with the kids."

"She was probably in bed with him." Donnie interjected sarcastically. I glared at him.

"Honey, you know I have to work in order to pay my rent. I am usually there before seven in the morning, until we close, five days a week."

Donnie interrupted again. "How much does she pay you?"

I breathed deeply, still trying to remain calm. "Clara can only afford minimum wage, but it's enough."

"Are you happy there mom?" Amy asked.

I thought for a second. "Yes I am. I enjoy working with Clara. She has become a good friend. But you are right, I haven't been available for you to drop your kids off during the day, but I am not going to apologize for that. From now on, I will make a point of seeing you and them on the weekends.

Why didn't you come and tell me how you were feeling? We could have worked something out. I don't know what you are thinking, if you don't tell me."

I held out my arms and both girls rushed into them. "This hasn't been easy on any of us and I understand how you feel.

From now on, we will make sure we have time for each other."

Donnie was pacing around the room like a caged animal. I hadn't seen him that agitated since he was a child. Back then I used to hold him and talk to him until he calmed down, but I knew that wouldn't work now. I also knew whatever he was going to say wasn't going to be good.

He turned and looked at me. "Are you sleeping with him?"

"I don't think that is any of your business. I don't go around asking you who you are sleeping with, do I?"

"So are you or aren't you?" he sneered at me.

"What do you think? That is enough young man. I am your mother and you don't have the right to talk to me this way."

"I can talk to you however I want. You don't have to answer me, it's written all over your face. You are nothing but a whore, spreading your legs for the first man who pays attention to you. He is using you. We know his kind – find a lonely widow and take her for everything she has."

"Jason isn't like that. Besides I don't have much for him to take, your dad made sure of that." I decided this wasn't the right time to tell them I had bought the cabin back.

Donnie had a lot more nasty things to say and his words made me feel cheap. He sounded so much like Jim it was unnerving. I didn't try to stop him. In a way, I felt I deserved his anger.

I can't remember exactly what he said, but he went too far. I don't know whatever possessed me but I walked up to him and slapped him across the face. "Don't you ever call me a whore again. You think your dad was so perfect, but you need to face reality. He hadn't made love to me for more than five years. I was left to pay his debts. I was forced to sell our house and find a way to support myself .He was cheating on me and left his lover everything that should have been ours. All I have left is you kids. My husband died and I am alone. Why can't you see that I have to build a new life for myself without him? He is dead, and he isn't coming back."

"Poor you," Donnie replied sarcastically. "I bet he is laughing and thanking his lucky stars he doesn't have to put up with you anymore. Especially now when you turned out to be exactly what he thought you were. He told me how you deliberately got pregnant and trapped him into having to marry you."

I went into shock. *Where was all of this anger coming from? Does he blame me because his father is dead? Did Jim actually tell him that or is Donnie saying whatever comes into his head?*

Angie spoke up. "That's enough Donnie. Stop bullying her. You are doing the same thing dad used to do. Mom is right. Life is too short to live alone."

"I want you to stop seeing him," Donnie demanded.

"Really," I replied. "Just who do you think you are,

telling me what to do?"

He looked me right in the eye and said, "It's him or us. You can't have it both ways."

"Are you seriously telling me I have to choose?"

Both girls were crying. "Please Donnie stop and think about what you are saying. It doesn't have to be this way," Amy begged.

"Donnie glared at her. "Shut up. I am the head of this family now. Your choice mom, him or us."

I felt my heart break in two. There were so many things I wanted to say. I wanted to beg Donnie not to force me into making this choice, but I didn't. I got out of the chair walked over and opened the door. My voice broke as I said "I love you" and walked out.

I was surprised to see Jason sitting in the car, waiting for me. I got in and stared straight ahead.

"Are you okay?" he asked softly.

"No I'm not and I don't think I ever will be again. Please take me home."

He reached for my hand, but I pulled it away. He got a strange look on his face, but didn't try again. I didn't want his comfort or understanding. I needed to try and figure out what happened .and why.

When we arrived at my apartment, he asked "do you want me to come up with you?" He leaned over to kiss me, but I turned my head away.

"Talk to me Lucy. What did they say to you?"

"I can't Jason. If you don't mind I need to be alone." I got out of the car, ran up the stairs and never looked back. Jason sat there for a long time before driving away.

When I got into my apartment, I sat on the couch. *How did my world ever come to this? I have lost everything and I don't know what I did to deserve this.*

* * *

Jason phoned early the next morning before I left for work. "I hated seeing you so upset. Did you manage to get any sleep last night?"

"No. I was awake most of the night."

"What happened after I left? One minute we are good, and the next you are freezing me out?"

I knew I had to tell him. "Donnie issued me an ultimatum, either you or them. If I choose them, I lose you. If I choose you, I lose my children and grandchildren…."

I heard him swear. "What are you going to do?"

"I don't know. I love you, but not seeing my grandchildren will kill me." I knew every word I said was hurting him.

"So are you telling me, you need some space to figure this out?"

"Do you mind – just a couple of days? I'm so confused right now, I can't think straight. Maybe Donnie will come to his senses, see what a terrible mistake he is making and apologize. I don't know what they expect me to do or say."

Jason suddenly got very quiet. "I'm not going to stay in the background and sneak around to see you behind their back."

"I don't want that," I replied, tears running down my face. "Jason please tell me what I should do."

"I can't, this is a decision you have to make for yourself, but you also need to know I won't wait forever."

"You're not being fair either. I'm not asking you to wait forever; all I am asking for is time to figure out what I can do.

"I know Lucy .Goodbye," he hung up.

I guess in my own way I was hoping he would give me the answer. No matter how this went, I stood to lose somebody I loved dearly. On top of that, I wasn't sure I would ever be able to forgive Donnie for forcing me into this situation. *He definitely is his father's son. This is something Jim would do and not think twice about the consequences.*

CHAPTER TWENTY FOUR

The next morning, Clara noticed something was wrong as soon as I walked in the door but I wasn't ready to talk to her. After the lunch rush she asked me "are ye going to tell me what's wrong with ye today? Ye look like ye lost yer best friend."

"I feel like have. Jason and I agreed I needed some space. I felt our relationship was moving too fast."

"This be yer idea or his?"

"I guess you could say it was a mutual agreement."

She gave me the look that means she thinks I am making a mistake, but said nothing more.

On every level of my being I knew Donnie was out of line by forcing me to choose between Jason and my kids, but I also knew this was a decision I had to make on my own. Either way I was going to hurt for a very long time.

In the end, I chose my family over Jason, and that was one of the hardest decisions I have made in my life. I loved him, but I loved my kids more. I knew I would eventually get over Jason but not being part of my grandchildren's lives would kill me. I guess, in a way, I was hoping I could have things both ways.

That evening, at the end of the meeting, I pulled Jason aside. "After everybody has left can we talk?"

"I was planning on coming to your place. Can it wait until then?"

I ignored his comment. "I'll wait over there for you." I couldn't look at him.

It seemed to take forever until the last person left, and he locked the door. I watched him walk over to me knowing that after tonight, I would be alone again.

"What's going on Lucy." he asked when he stopped in front of me, "the ice queen is back."

This time I knew exactly what he meant. At first I couldn't get the words out. I didn't want to break his heart, but better now than later.

He put his hand under my chin and stared into my eyes. "How about you start at the beginning and tell me what is going on.

Before the tears began I managed to say, "I can't see you anymore."

"What? Why? I don't understand. I love you and you said you loved me."

"I do love you. That's what makes this so hard. My children…."

"What about your children. What do they have to do with this?"

I took a deep breath. "I have already told you that they gave me an ultimatum that I have to choose between you and them. If I choose to be with you, they will have nothing more to do with me. I won't even be allowed to see my grandchildren"

Jason swore. "I don't have to guess who is behind this. Donnie right?"

I nodded my head in agreement.

"What are his reasons or does he even have any?"

"He thinks I am too old for you and he doesn't like the idea of us being together. He has put his dad on a pedestal. He thinks he was the perfect father, and I am tarnishing his image. Jason, please try to understand, he is grieving and afraid of losing me too."

"Damn him," Jason swore again. "So you have decided to let your adult children dictate how you are going to live the rest of your life."

"I guess so." I answered. I knew he was hurt and angry. I put my hand on his arm but he shook it off. "I am sorry Jason. I do love you, but they haven't left me much choice."

"You had a choice Lucy," he said bitterly, "and you made it. I came out second best."

I wanted to tell him that wasn't true but didn't. He was right. "Please try and understand Jason. I don't want this, but I don't know what else to do."

Without saying another word he walked over to the

door, unlocked it, and held it open for me. "You had belter go home before I say a lot of things I don't mean. I also suggest you don't attend any more meetings. The strain between us will only make the others feel uncomfortable. Go, I have to lock up." His eyes and voice were cold. "You can gather the few things I have at your apartment and leave them outside the door. I'll pick them up later."

I grabbed his arm, "Jason, please try to understand."

"No Lucy, there is nothing to understand. It's over because that is what you want, not me."

"I do love you," I said to him, my eyes begging for understanding.

"Apparently not enough and I doubt very much that your children have any idea what you are sacrificing for them."

There was nothing left to say. I walked out the door and sat in my car, staring straight ahead. A few minutes later he came out, locked the door, got on his motorcycle and rode way. I watched until his taillight disappeared. *I know I made the right choice, but why does it feel so wrong?*

I was awake most of the night, searching for a way out of this situation, but came up with nothing. I realized that, even if I came up with a solution, Jason wouldn't take me back. The hurt I inflicted was too deep.

The next morning Clara took one look at me and shook her head, "Ye look awful today. I'm afraid ye'll scare away the customers."

"Only one, Jason and I broke up last night."

She didn't say a word. In fact she ignored me the rest of the day unless she had to answer a question. I was miserable. I kept hoping Jason would walk in and we could talk this over, but of course he didn't.

We were closing up when she scolded me, "If'n yer going to do this, ye' need to realize yer children are going to go about their own lives, and yer going to grow old alone. That is the choice yer makin'. If'n ye let yer kids tell you how to live yer life ye'll be making the biggest mistake ye ever made. That's the choice yer making, but is that what ye want?"

"Clara, that's not the way it is. They will get over whatever this is. Then maybe Jason and I will have a chance."

"Yes, it is and ye don't have enough sense to see what's right in front of ye. Maybe ye need to think about someone else besides yerself for a change. Jason loves ye but he isn't the kind of man to wait around in case ye decide to change yer mind. Ah well, won't do me much good to say any more. Ye be making' year bed, and now ye'll have to lie in it."

CHAPTER TWENTY FIVE

Shortly after we broke up there was a brief period of time when I thought I might be pregnant. Age forty-two was not when I would have chosen to have another baby. I didn't have that worry while Jim was alive, because of his secret vasectomy. I wanted more children but Jim made his choice and now I understood why.

If I am pregnant I can deal with it. I will have a reminder of the love Jason and I shared, but a few days later I found out I wasn't. Part of me was relieved, the other part devastated. Now he was lost to me completely.

I hadn't seen or heard from Jason for several months. He stopped coming for his morning coffee and, as he requested, I stopped going to the meetings. I came home after work, watched television, and went to bed. Most nights I slept poorly. The next morning I got up and went to work, did my job and repeated the process. I was depressed but didn't care.

I lost weight and ignored the fact that I needed a haircut. Cee Cee did her best to cheer me up until I told her to leave me alone. I was miserable and didn't care who knew it.

Every two weeks Clara packed up a box of cookies to take to the group and asked me if I wanted to go with her. Each time I said no.

The first anniversary of Jim's passing arrived and I decided to take a bouquet of flowers to the cemetery. To me it was just another day to get through. When I arrived I saw the children had been there. The girls left small bouquets of flowers and Donnie must have left the open bottle of beer. I'm not sure why, but I am sure he had his reason.

I knelt down and placed my flowers on his grave, said a prayer, then left. If I thought losing Jim was hard, losing Jason was tearing me apart. I remained dry eyed because I knew that once I started crying I wouldn't be able to stop. The two men I loved were gone from my life and I hurt more than I ever thought possible. I recognized the fact I was going through the grieving process again but this time there would be no happy ending.

I spent as much time as possible with my grandchildren. To tell the truth, they are the only thing that kept me sane during this time. I found it easier to be with my girls, as we had more in common. By mutual agreement we didn't discuss the ugly scene which had taken place that day

I hadn't seen or heard from Donnie since that evening, which was just as well. I didn't want to fight any more. I told myself he would eventually get over what was bothering him or else be a long time mad," but that didn't make my life any easier. He stayed in contact with the girls and they kept me up to date on his comings and goings. As far as I knew, he was still angry with me.

I existed. In some ways being apart from Jason was worse than dealing with Jim's death. I loved Jim when he was alive, but I was in love with Jason.

All of this changed one day when I was babysitting for Amy while she went shopping. When she got home she asked "Can you stay a little longer? Do you think we could talk?"

"Sure, I'm not in a hurry anyway." I dreaded the thought of going back to my apartment.

I followed her into the kitchen. She made us some tea and busied herself putting the groceries away. The next time I looked her shoulders were shaking and she was sobbing.

I walked over to her and put my arm around her. "What's the matter Amy?" I asked gently. Of the two girls, Amy was the most emotional and sensitive.

"I'm worried about you," she finally stuttered out.

"About me? Why?"

"Look at you. You are losing weight. There are dark circles under your eyes and you never smile any more. Are you sick and not telling us?"

"No Amy, I am fine, just going through a rough patch. You have nothing to worry about." *I wanted to scream at her I am not fine. I miss Jason and I am angry that I allowed my children to put me in this prison.* But, as mothers often do, I said nothing.

"Mom, I'm sorry."

"About what? I don't see where you have anything to be sorry about."

"Did you like that Jason guy?"

"Yes, very much, but that has been over for a long time." Tears filled my eyes, but I wasn't going to let her see me cry.

"Mom, tell me about you and dad. Not what we saw on the surface, but what was really going on between the two of you."

Now that I had the opportunity I didn't know how much to say. I wasn't sure what she wanted to hear.

"I loved your dad, but he tended to be very controlling, especially when it came to money. Being a father was very important to him. He wanted to be there for you kids.'

"Did you ever want to have a job?"

"Yes, but he wouldn't allow it. He would tell me "I make the money; your job is to look after the family." I kept myself busy doing what I could. I helped at the school, volunteered for your sports clubs – I am sure you remember what I always did."

"Were you happy?"

"I thought I was," I replied.

"How was your sex life mom, with dad being gay and all of that?"

"That's a little personal don't you think?"

"For goodness sake mom, I'm a married woman with children of my own. I do know how babies are made. I would be naïve to think that you and dad didn't have sex once in a while."

I felt my face turn red. I wasn't sure I wanted to have this conversation with my daughter.

"Mom, I am asking because I am trying to understand."

I took a deep breath. "I guess you could say it was normal until after Donnie was born. After that, your dad seemed to lose interest. Over the years it became less and less, until we finally stopped."

"When was that mom?" she asked gently.

"About five or six years before he died, I'm not sure any more."

She thought for a moment and then asked "did you ever suspect he was gay?"

"No, not until he passed away. I thought his disinterest was normal after being married for such a long time. A lot of things became clearer after he died."

"How do you feel about dad now?"

"He was my first love, my husband for twenty-five years, and the father of my children. I loved him for that, but I don't know if I was in love with him all that time. Now, I think of how conflicted he must have been, and having control over his home and family was his way of proving who he was."

"Tell me about Jason mom."

"There isn't much to tell, He is gentle, warm and compassionate. After his girlfriend and his daughter died he formed the Bereavement group as a way of helping others.

He was good to me. He made me laugh. I did things I had never done before, like go bowling, going to a country bar, learning how to line dance, going for my first ride on a motorcycle and riding in his convertible with the wind in my hair. When a person gets married at sixteen, there isn't time to have experienced much of life. As you kids got older I had dreams of going to different places and trying different things, but that's all they were. The time we went to Mexico was the only holiday your dad and I had. He didn't enjoy himself very much and after that fiasco your dad refused to go on another trip."

"Why Jason mom? He looks like one of those bikers you see on television. He has that bad boy vibe about him.

"I guess, in a way, that's the way he is. He is also a gifted, skilled, grievance counsellor, a successful business man and a talented musician. Amy, we can't judge people by how they look, on the outside, we have to get to know who they are on the inside. Jason is a good man and probably far better than I deserve."

"Do you miss him mom?"

"Yes, very much."

We were both quiet for a while and then she asked, "What about Donnie? Do you hate him?"

"No, I could never do that, but I can honestly say I don't

like him much right now. Love and like are totally different concepts. I think he is still trying to understand his dad and is afraid Jason will try to step in and try to take his place. He is just as bull-headed as your dad was, but now, saying he's sorry won't be easy. I also think he sees his role as man of the family and that we should all listen to him, but in actuality he is still a little boy missing his father. He has to figure this out for himself.

Try not to worry about me okay. I am a survivor and will survive this too. One day all will be good again. I promise."

She came over and hugged me. "Mom maybe you should try and explain how you feel to Angie and Donnie. This is tearing you apart."

"One day I will but not right now. I'm not ready yet and don't want to fight anymore.'

'I wish I could be more like you," she confessed.

"No you don't. My world is full of hurt and disillusionment right now, and I don't want that for you."

A short while later I went back to my apartment. I knew I had said too much to her, but on the other hand, my children needed to know their parents were human and had their own faults. For the first time in months my heart felt a little lighter, and I felt better than I had for a long time.

The next day, as usual, Clara and I stopped for a break after the lunch rush.

"Jason asked about ye last night when I brought the cookies to 'im."

"Oh, and what did you tell him?"

"I said ye look like crap and that the two of ye need to fix this."

"Clara, please don't worry about me. We are over. I made my choice, and as much as it hurts, that's the way it is."

"I bin worried about ye. Why even the customers are asking if yer sick."

"My daughter asked me the same thing the other day, but I am fine. I'm just not sleeping very well."

Clara stood up and put her hands on her hips. "Did anyone ever tell you that yer both too stubborn for yer own good? Yer both hurtin each other when there be no need for it."

"Clara, stop! It is what it is."

She turned and stomped away, muttering to herself. I got up, cleared off our table and wiped off all of the others. I looked at the clock. *I can put up with her silence for three more hours. Better that then listening to her tell me about my mistakes. I already know what they are and I don't need her to remind me.*

CHAPTER TWENTY SIX

Sunday, my one day to relax, was usually long and unproductive. I was still in my pajamas and housecoat enjoying my coffee when someone began pounding on my door.

"Lucy, open this door before I break it down," Jason shouted.

I opened the door and stared at him. "What are you doing here?"

The look on his face unnerved me. Only once before had I seen him look so fierce and determined.

"Get dressed," he barked at me. "You are coming with me."

"I am not going anywhere with you," and I moved to slam the door shut. "Who do you think you are barging in here after all these months and telling me what to do?" He put out his foot and stopped the door from closing.

"Fine, either you get dressed or I will take you the way you are. It's up to you."

We stood there practically nose to nose staring at each other. I flinched first. "Okay, okay I need a few minutes." I was furious. *Just who does he think he is walking in here and ordering me around?*

I stalked into my bedroom, and quickly dressed, grabbing the first pair of jeans and sweater I saw in my closet, When I walked back in to the living room he took my hand and practically dragged me out the door and down the stairs to his car. I got in my side and he walked around to the other.

When he slammed his door shut I asked, "What do you think you are doing? After months of silence you think you can come and bully me?"

He muttered something about damn stubborn women and he was tired of living like a monk, and that was going to end today, come hell or high water.

"Where are we going?" I asked.

"You will see when we get there."

His hands were tight on the steering wheel and he never said a word as we drove across town.

"Turn this car around right now, and take me home," I demanded. "I don't like the way you are treating me." He ignored me.

He turned onto Amy's street and parked across the driveway, blocking Donnie's truck from leaving.

"Amy invited us for brunch."

"Why didn't you say so, instead of acting like a cave man?"

"You wouldn't have come."

I felt the panic rising in me. The last thing I wanted was to be part of a confrontation between Jason and Donnie. "I can't do this. I don't want to go inside."

He turned and looked at me. "Please Lucy this can't continue the way it is. The longer this, whatever it is, goes on, the smaller the chance of healing. Besides, I need you in my life." Then he   got out of the car, came around to my side and opened the door.

"Stop and give me a minute," I begged. Instead he grabbed my hand, and literally dragged me down the sidewalk and up the stairs to the door.

My heart was racing, my hands were clammy and I was struggling to catch my breath. I thought I was going to faint. The urge to run as far away as I could, was overpowering.

He ignored me and rang the doorbell. Seconds later, Amy opened the door.

"Good you came," she said then put her arms around me and gave me a hug. "It will be okay," she whispered in my ear.

To Jason she said," we are in the kitchen."

Jason and I followed her. "Mom's and Jason are here," she announced.

Donnie and Angie were laughing about something. When he looked over, and saw Jason he stopped.

"What are you doing here? Nobody invited you" he sneered at Jason.

"That's where you are wrong," Amy rebuked him. "I invited him."

"As far as I am concerned he can leave any time. In fact I will be glad to show him to the door."

Jason looked at him calmly, "Sit down and shut up."

This is not going to be good. "I think it would be better for me to wait outside," I said, and scurried back to the door.

"Good idea," Jason replied.

Amy and Angie were speechless. Very few people have had the nerve to speak to Donnie that way.

In fact I couldn't get out of there fast enough. I got as far as the steps then sat down on the top one, trying to calm myself. I didn't want to hear what was being said inside.

As soon as the door closed behind me, Jason turned to them. He addressed them in a steady controlled voice, "You guys should be ashamed of yourselves for the way you are treating your mother.

Don't you think she has been through enough this past year? Yet, not once have I heard her complain or say a derogatory thing about your dad. Not once has she complained about her job and its low pay. The customers and Clara love her.

She is still a young vibrant woman and learning to experience what you take for granted. You are depriving her of a chance to do and be somebody. She raised you to who you are today, what more can you ask of her?"

Then he turned to Donnie. "You have no right to call her names. Did any of you know she's had never been bowling, or to a country bar, or had a ride in a convertible? Of course you didn't, because you never bothered to ask. You have been too wrapped in your own little worlds to see how much she is hurting

How can I make you understand what you are doing to her? Your mom is like a butterfly coming out of her cocoon into the world, and you are stopping her. If the butterfly can't complete its emergence it withers and dies but, if it spreads its wings and learns how to fly, the world becomes a better place. Is that what you want for her? "

"Really," Donnie sneered, "that's the best you can come up with?"

Jason's hands curled into fists, but he kept them tight by his side. He told me later it was all he could do to keep from punching Donnie in the face.

Angie spoke up. "He's right Donnie. You know what you are asking of her is wrong."

"How do you figure that? She is a mom, and mom's don't ride motorcycles or sleep with men they hardly know. They stay home and raise their kids."

"And what happens when the kids are raised, your husband is dead and you are alone?" Jason asked quietly. "What do you do then? Do you live in the past or try to build a new future?"

Donne got a puzzled look on his face. "I don't know. I

175

never thought about it."

"I'll tell you. She finds someone who loves her as much as I do and you give her your blessing to be happy again. Your mom has done her duty. She raised you, and now like the butterfly she needs to spread her wings and learn how to fly.

She doesn't stop being your mom. Her world didn't stop because your dad died. She has to go on living and you need to let her."

"And what we become one big happy family?" Donnie asked sarcastically.

"We could be a family if you give us a chance Donnie. The very idea of forcing her to choose between you and me was grossly unfair. Well guess what, she chose you and now you need to appreciate what she has given up."

Looking at Donnie he continued. "I understand you haven't made any kind of effort to see or talk to her since that evening. Why is that? Your mom hasn't stopped loving you but the longer you let this go on, the deeper the rift will become."

Without giving Donnie a chance to reply he added. "I love your mom and I intend to marry her. Your mom and I are going to be together whether you like it or not. Now you have to choose whether you want to be in our life, or not." He paused for several seconds to let his words sink in. "Doesn't feel very good does it?"

By now Donnie was openly crying. "I'm sorry. I didn't

mean to hurt her. I never thought…."

"That's right, you didn't think," Jason said.

Angie walked over and put her arms around her brother. "I think mom is probably outside some place. Maybe you need to go and talk to her."

When Donnie came outside, I was still sitting on the top step. He sat down beside me and I put my arm around him. He put his head on my shoulder and cried. I held him for a long time, neither of us saying a word.

Finally I asked, "Is it safe to go inside?"

"Mom I'm sorry. I didn't deliberately set out to hurt you. I am mad at dad yet I don't want anybody else to take his place."

"Jason wouldn't try to take over your dad's place. He understands we come as a package deal. Maybe you could learn to see him as a friend, not as a rival for my affection."

"He loves you."

"I know, and I love him."

"He wants to marry you."

"That I have to think about – maybe further down the line. I'm not ready to make that kind of commitment just yet."

"It's okay if you do mom, but if he ever hurts you, he will have to answer to me," and then he looked up at me.

"Are we good now?"

"Yes, but on one condition. You have to let me live my life the same as I have to let you. Oh, and I have another idea, maybe you could think about coming to the next Bereavement group meeting with me."

"Not sure about that one mom."

I stood up and held out my hand. "How about we go inside and eat. I'm starving."

He laughed, took my hand and we walked into the house together. *No matter how old my children are they still need me to be there for them.*

EPILOGUE

I wish I could say "and they lived happily ever after," but this is a story about life, in its rawest emotional form. We compromised, we forgave, we argued, we laughed and we cried together.

Donnie and Jason learned to get along. Amy and Angie are crazy about Jason and he loves being a step-grandfather. We are engaged and planning on getting married in the spring. I moved out of my apartment into his house, but chose to keep my job with Clara.

One evening, shortly after I moved in, I was sitting on the deck watching the sun go down. Jason came out and handed me a glass of wine.

"What are you thinking about?" he asked "You look so serious."

"I was thinking about Jim. I hope he is happy wherever he is. In his own way, he left a legacy which has taught us how to acceptance of our differences, and shown us the power of love and forgiveness."

I lifted my glass of wine to the stars shining in the heavens. *"Thank you Jim,"* I whispered from my heart.

ABOUT THE AUTHOR

Judy lives with her husband Bob and they have four children, five grandsons and the head of the house, their dog Missy. When Judy retired from the business world she decided to chase her dream of writing a book. This is the eleventh book where she has attempted to take the problems facing women today and offer encouragement.

You can reach her at jcoates@telusplanet.net